D1325214

Also by Elizabeth Hawkins

The Maze

Sea of Peril

Elizabeth Hawkins

 ORCHARD BOOKS

To Rupert

Orchard Books
96 Leonard Street, London EC2A 4RH
Orchard Books Australia
14 Mars Road, Lane Cove, NSW 2066
1 86039 041 2 (hardback)
1 86039 065 X (paperback)
First published in Great Britain 1995
First paperback publication 1996
Text © Elizabeth Hawkins 1995
The right of Elizabeth Hawkins to be identified as the
Author of this Work has been asserted by her in
accordance with the Copyright, Designs and Patents Act, 1988.

A CIP catalogue record for this book is available from the
British Library.

Printed in Great Britain.

CHAPTER ONE

"Well, I'll be –! Listen to this!" Jimmy's father thumped the paper that lay beside him on the table.

Jimmy started and choked over his hot tea.

"You all right, Jimmy?" said his mother anxiously. "Have a good cough and bring it up. Burnt yer throat, has it? You shouldn't be in so much of a hurry." Her hand landed on his back. "Go on – cough it up."

Two hands gripped Jimmy's shoulders and shook him.

"Leave it, Mum. I'm all right," he gasped, tears streaming down his face.

Through the tears Jimmy could see his father's watery outline, his finger moving along the lines of newsprint, his mouth silently spelling out the words. He looked up briefly and caught Jimmy's eye, before concentrating on the paper again.

"Leave him be, Ethel. No need to fuss over him."

The tea was too hot. You had to drink it hot because cold it tasted like dishwater, with the stuff you got with rationing. But it hadn't been the tea so much as the surprise.

Dad wasn't often home for tea. Jimmy never knew when he'd be back. He might be called to take a goods

1

train up north, or a trainload of sailors down to Plymouth. Security, his father said. If he worked to a predictable timetable the Germans could find out and his precious cargoes would be a sitting duck for the German bombers.

It hadn't happened. War had been declared a year ago, and they'd all got keyed up with endless warnings on the wireless to be prepared. But nothing had come of it. Jimmy had given up scanning the skies each night. He was longing to spot a German Junker 88, or even a Heinkel bomber but the Jerries seemed to like their sleep and warm beds as much as Dad and Mum did.

And today Dad had shown up, unexpectedly, for tea.

Mum had wiped the oilcloth, put the bread and marge on a nice plate, and tonight they had a tin of ham and some tomatoes from Dad's pot in the yard. Dad sat reading the evening paper while Mum and Jimmy ate in silence.

"Yer father's had a hard day at work, Jimmy," Mum warned him. "He'll talk when it suits him."

Usually Dad didn't talk until he'd folded up the paper and laid it beside his plate. Jimmy liked that – at least his mother couldn't ask him questions.

But tonight Dad had spoken and he'd only started on the first page. That was why Jimmy had been so surprised.

"Ethel – listen to this."

"Yes, Reg."

Mum wasn't listening. She was still staring anxiously

at Jimmy. As he caught her eye she gave him her quick are-you-sure-you're-all right smile.

"The Canadian government has offered to take children at risk from bombin' in the cities and find them good homes in Canada until the end of the war."

"So . . .? What do you mean?" Jimmy's mother said in a strained voice.

"It says here, 'Why should the children of the rich pay their way to safety in America? All children in need should have their chance to survive.'"

"But we're not in need, Reg. We're makin' do nicely. And there 'ent been much bombin'. I reckon it's too far for the Jerries to make it across the Channel."

"It's goin' to come, Ethel. It stands to reason. And that great reservoir at the back, next to the engine sheds, it stands out like a beacon. Bright as a mirror on a good night."

"Come on, Reg!" Mum pretended to laugh. "Who'd bomb a reservoir?"

"It's the engine sheds beside it they'd go for. Disrupt the trains and the troop transport. The reservoir is on all the maps. It's a marker, like. We're in the path here, Ethel, and you can't deny it."

Mum stared desperately at Jimmy. Jimmy stared back pretending not to understand. Of course he did, and he hated it.

"He's all we've got . . . No, Reg! He's all God's left us."

It had been like this a year ago, when his mother had refused to allow him to be evacuated to the country. Dad had been angry, saying she was only thinking of herself and not of Jimmy. Jimmy had felt disappointed not to see the countryside, but most of his friends had come back after a few months and said it was a right muddle, nothing organised, and the country families hadn't wanted them and said they had no manners.

But still, he hadn't liked being treated differently. As far as he was concerned his two elder brothers, who had died of meningitis before he was born, had let him down.

As for his youngest brother, Peter, he could only remember him coughing as a baby. But he could remember his little sister. He'd loved her. She'd had fair curls so soft he'd sometimes stroked them, and when he tickled her she giggled with a big gap where her front teeth had come out. She'd died too – measles or something. He didn't like to remember.

"It says here: 'Mr Geoffrey Shakespeare MP, Under-Secretary for the Dominions, has formed a Children's Overseas Reception Board (CORB) to select children, equip them, organise their passage overseas and then find each child a suitable billet in Canada with good care, supervision and education.'"

Dad put the paper down and stared across at Jimmy. His eyes were troubled as if he was struggling to understand something. Jimmy stared back as blankly as he could.

"It's because he's our only one, Ethel. We've a duty to give him a chance."

Mum was beginning to cry.

"He'll come back to us safe and well, and soon enough, Ethel," said his father softly. "Come on, Ethel. Do we have a choice?"

Jimmy's mother stood up abruptly and clattered the plates off into the sink. She turned back sharply, wiping her eyes with the skirt of her pinafore.

Behind him Jimmy felt her hesitate, then a hand smoothed down the wiry tufts on his head. Usually he shook it off. Tonight he sat like a statue.

"I'll write to this Mr Shakespeare, then," came her stifled whisper.

"Yes – you write best," agreed his father.

Then the tears came.

As Dad got up and moved towards Mum, Jimmy pushed his chair back and fled to his room.

With his head in his hands, his arms resting on the windowsill, he stared out at the shining blackness of the reservoir. Canada. Cor blimey! He didn't mind that.

Canada wasn't mentioned again. For the rest of the summer term Jimmy set out each morning with his gas mask over one shoulder and his school bag over the other.

Canada – what he'd give to go there!

All that prairie and the mountains, he'd seen them in his geography book. Jimmy could hardly imagine it as he trudged down Union Street.

Union Street had one line of tall terraced houses backing on to the reservoir, with a facing row of identical houses on the other side. At one end of the street were the engine sheds and at the other a crossing road of yet more terraced houses. They didn't even have front gardens, as steps led up from the street to their front doors, and down from the street to the basements.

The only wide open space was up – the sky. Jimmy tried to imagine a mountain where the engine sheds were. It didn't fit.

"Won't you miss yer mam and dad?" said Madge Watson. A spindly girl, she sat behind him in class and listened in to Jimmy's conversations with Bob, his desk partner.

"Don't be so nosy – we wasn't talking to you," said Bob.

"I'd miss me mam and dad," went on Madge. "Wouldn't you, Doreen? I mean they might get killed or somethin' while I was away, a bomb could fall on their heads . . ." She sniffed. She could cry at the drop of a hat.

"Don't be daft," muttered Bob. "If you stayed you 'ud be dead with them.

Jimmy felt guilty. He wanted to go to Canada so much he knew he wouldn't miss his mum and dad. One of the reasons he wanted to go was to get away from them. He loved them, he knew that, but they loved him back too much. Every time he got a cold,

6

Mum was up half the night making him hot drinks. It was plain she expected him to die any minute – like the others. She couldn't leave him alone, always persuading him to have a bit of her butter ration, "No, really, Jimmy – I don't want it. You're the growing lad."

It was embarrassing. Most of the families in Union Street had too many mouths to feed. You had to fight for every bit you could get. Yet in his home Mum was forcing food down him. He'd much rather have had the chance to pinch and shove for it, like in Bob's house.

Dad was all right. He pretended not to care and bring his son up like everyone else, but Jimmy often caught him watching – that worried look.

Canada – he would breathe there. There was enough room.

"If they fancy you," went on Madge, "they'll keep you for years. They'll not give you back."

"Fancy, Jimmy!" said Bob and he rolled round the desk in silent laughter.

"Mebbe if they don't like him they'll keep him a slave . . ."

"Who is that talking?" Miss Wellington's voice boomed down the rows of desks. "Bob Baynham and Jimmy Smith – get on with your fractions."

All heads bowed to the desks.

"My dad says you're a coward if you runs from the war," Doreen's icy whisper floated through from behind. "We're all in danger, he says, and we've to face it together, like."

Doreen's words were like a stab in the back. Jimmy hadn't thought of that.

"Think I'd be a coward if I went?" Jimmy asked his father.

Dad had been away two nights taking trains up to Glasgow and back. They had had their tea and Mum was tearing up newspaper into squares, threading them on string. She'd slipped out to hang them in the toilet in the yard.

"Where's that, Jimmy?" his father asked.

"Canada."

It was the first time Canada had been mentioned since that night in May.

"Canada, Jimmy?" Dad laughed. "Do you know how many families applied for their children? Thousands and thousands. Forget it, son. And, no, you wouldn't be a coward. Where's this country goin' to be if we don't save the next generation?"

Jimmy went up to bed dumbstruck. He had wanted to go so badly he couldn't believe he didn't have a chance. He stayed awake until it grew dark watching the anti-aircraft lights sweeping across the sky. Not a German plane in sight. It was all phoney this war, everyone telling you to be careful, to carry your gas mask everywhere, to practise filing into the cellar of the empty warehouse at the end of the street that had been turned into a shelter.

Even Grandad had volunteered for the Local Defence Corps. Good thing he lived two streets over. Jimmy had seen them drilling, not a gun among them, Grandad limping with his arthritis, with a chair leg that he'd sharpened at one end held to his shoulder. Old Mr Hodge, Grandad's mate from the pub, carried a broom for a weapon. What did he think he'd do – sweep the Germans away?

Now Canada . . . Had that been another 'let's pretend' plan?

If he could hold his breath while the searchlight swept back and forward across the sky, Canada would be real.

Jimmy sucked in his breath. The light moved like a giant torch across the sky – he was bursting – the light crossed another light moving in the opposite direction and swung back – he was going to fall on his bed. Then the beam fell back and Jimmy let out a gasp. He'd done it!

"Oh no!"

Jimmy was woken by the cry.

"No!"

Jimmy leapt out of bed and down the stairs. His mother was standing in front of the door, bending over, clasping something to her chest. At her feet lay a brown envelope. Jimmy could make out the bold, black writing at the top: ON HIS MAJESTY'S SERVICE, CORB.

"What's up, Mum?"

"Never you mind."

His mother turned and scurried into the kitchen, but not before he saw the white letter shoved under her pinafore. She moved towards the stove.

"Is Dad here?"

"He's been called out again."

His mother was bending over the range, as if in pain.

"What's it say, Mum? Am I goin' to Canada or ain't I?"

His mother gasped and Jimmy knew he had guessed right. With a sigh she pulled out the white letter and laid it down on the table. It wouldn't go in the range now, he guessed. His mother's hand was trembling. Jimmy edged his fingers towards her over the table and she gripped and held his hand.

"Make me a cup of tea, Jimmy," she said as she sank into her chair.

It was the best summer holidays any of them had ever had on Union Street. The children were left to themselves. Older ones looked after young ones and no one checked up on them. There wasn't the time. Fathers came back from work, had their tea and then went off to their volunteer war jobs as firemen, or air-raid wardens. Younger men were being called into the forces, leaving their jobs, and unmarried girls were

10

working long hours in the factories to take their places, but they were still short of workers.

Now the mothers were disappearing from Union Street too. Before, the doorsteps had been littered with mothers in cloth turbans, shaking their dusters, yelling at the children or slopping out buckets into the gutters in the street. You couldn't get away with anything without being seen by someone. Precious few mothers had worked before, but even Jimmy's mum, who was forever saying "A woman's place is in the home", had taken a part-time job in the parachute factory in the next street.

Before the war it had been Rothstein's Ladies' Lingerie factory, where all the unmarried girls sat at sewing machines, making brassières and corsets. Jimmy knew, because he and the other boys shinned up the drainpipe to peep through the windows and giggle at the rows of girls at their machines, sewing "unmentionables". Mr Rothstein owned the place and ran it as a modern lingerie business, but now the government had decided it was the ideal place to change over from making silk camiknickers to making silk parachutes.

Mum came home happy and full of stories from the factory. She fussed less over Jimmy and tried out new recipes she'd swapped at work. How to make cakes with no eggs or sugar, or some such.

Jimmy, Bob and their gang explored the engine sheds, running away when they were spotted, or mucked around the reservoir, or played football up and

11

down Union Street. When they smashed a window at old Mrs Busby's no one even heard them. They'd never have got away with it before.

The next day they did all feel a bit bad and went to help Mrs Busby put a board over her window and reassured her it wasn't a German bomb, just their ball.

Dad sat by the crackling wireless set when he was home, and listened to the distant, posh voices of the announcers reporting occasional bombs dropped on airfields or naval ports and relaying the German advance through the Low Countries, Holland and Belgium, and finally through the French defences and on towards the English Channel.

So it wasn't until the holidays were over, 7 September 1940, that the war finally arrived on Union Street.

CHAPTER TWO

"Jimmy, just run round to the baker's, will you, love? If yer father's back we'll not have enough bread for the weekend."

Jimmy had come in for his tea after a glorious afternoon playing by the reservoir with Bob. The sun shone in a clear blue sky and, if the autumn term hadn't started at school, you'd have thought it was still summer.

"Get me a square tin loaf and have it cut and put in a bag. And watch how you go comin' back – I want every slice of that loaf untouched, do you hear?"

Jimmy grinned.

Now he carried the brown bag home, kicking a tin can he'd found in the street. His fingers itched. He was just working his forefinger and thumb into the bag, fingering the crust, when the sirens started. Another test – there'd been plenty of tests before.

Jimmy kicked the can as the wailing built up to a shrill pitch. It went on and on and on . . . And there was a droning, like an annoying fly. Jimmy glanced back over his shoulder. He could see the flies behind him, swarms in the blue sky, wave after wave of little black blobs.

"Don't stand dreamin', son!" shrieked an old woman hurrying past with her shopping bag. "Looks as if they're comin' an' all."

Coming? The Germans coming? He stood, face upturned, watching. German bombers? A strange thrill of excitement flashed through him, like an electric shock. The wailing didn't die, but moaned on and on.

From either side of the street, doors were flung open and people burst out, running and yelling. It seemed as if the whole street had woken up together on this sleepy Saturday afternoon.

"Get into your shelter, boy," a man in a suit, hurrying past, called out. "Get off the street!"

Jimmy jerked round, as if from a trance, and grabbed his can from the dirt. Mum – why hadn't he thought of her? Where was she? He wedged the bag under his arm and tore down Middle Lane and round the corner into Union Street. Overhead the droning was coming closer.

Down Union Street he raced, dodging in and out of the people hurrying towards the old warehouse that was the street's official shelter.

"Jimmy!" his mother yelled as he reached the steps. "I was that worried!"

Jimmy grinned with relief. She was there – Mum had been standing at the top of the steps, watching for him. She turned, wiped her floury hands on her pinafore, locked the front door and scurried down.

"Come on, Jimmy!"

14

On all sides people were hurrying to the warehouse at the end of the street.

The guns had started – ack-ack . . .

Jimmy looked up to the sky and saw a fly fall, glinting in the sunlight, diving headlong. It exploded in a ball of white light and black smoke. The sky was like a huge cinema screen with Jimmy sitting below in the audience.

"Don't you dare run away, you little beggar," Mrs Williams from number 24 yelled at her Tommy. A little lad, he had run over to say hello to Jimmy. "Come back 'ere this minute!"

Tommy was firmly slapped and yanked along by the hand. His wails added to the moaning of the siren.

George Munro, who lived upstairs, above Jimmy and his parents, was helping his old mother. Dragging her, rather, as she limped along clutching her stick.

"Come on, Mother! We're nearly there – best foot forward."

Old Mrs Munro groaned quietly to herself.

As they reached the entrance to the warehouse, the ground shook and shuddered. Jimmy's mother grabbed his arm as a shrill whine came down from the sky, followed by a shattering explosion.

Suddenly Jimmy felt sick, blinded by a bright light.

"Come on, Jimmy! We've got to have somethin' safe over our heads."

They stumbled down stone steps into the warehouse as around them people pushed and shoved their way into the cramped cellars. They'd never all get in. But they did – somehow.

Jimmy listened to the droning of the aircraft overhead, broken by the dull, repeated thuds of the anti-aircraft guns. Explosions and crashes shook the floor beneath their feet. He was frightened, terrified. It was all right seeing it from a distance, but the blinding flash, the ground shaking beneath his feet, petrified him. Any moment the ground might yawn open and swallow them all up. He had waited so long to sight his first German bomber, but now he didn't want to look any longer. All he wanted to do was to bury his ears in his hands.

The cellar was stifling. For windows there were just two high openings crossed with iron bars. With so many bodies crammed in together there was a stink of sweat.

"It ain't right bringin' that dog in 'ere. Disgustin' – pets ain't allowed."

"Get off my foot, you fat slob! Get off, do you hear?"

"I'm not standin' on your blimmin' foot."

"Yes you are – oh, you get on my nerves, you do."

Outside, the guns had settled into a rhythmic thudding followed by a lull. Jimmy felt his head sagging in the heat.

"What's that boy doin' on a seat at his age? Get up! Who does he think he is – Mister High and Mighty?"

Mrs Best from two doors down, all spiky elbows and

bony knees, pulled Jimmy across a pram with a sleeping baby in. The baby woke up and started to shriek in Jimmy's ear.

"Let's have a song," called out a woman. She was in some kind of uniform. "Come on, everyone, now – Roll out the barrel . . ." The woman's voice trilled round the shelter. One or two young girls half-heartedly joined in.

"Shut yer bleedin' row," bellowed a man's voice from the side. "We's got enough noise with these bleedin' bombs without you lot."

The singing faltered and died out.

In the lulls Jimmy examined his tin can. He tried to push the dents out with his thumbnail, but his hands were trembling. Finally his mother grabbed him and pulled him to her. A low siren outside was rising to one continuous high note. All around there were yells of relief and cheers.

"It's the all-clear, Jimmy," smiled Mum.

The shoving and pushing started again as they opened the door to the street. People walked a few steps and stood and stared. There were cries and screams. Jimmy couldn't believe it. Smoke was billowing to the sky, shutting off the sun, and the heat was terrible. Flames shot up from one of the engine sheds at the end of the street. Several of the houses had been reduced to skeletons with missing walls, and beds half hanging out from the sloping bedrooms. One house had collapsed like a paper cut-out. Other houses had windows blown out and many had glass shattered, but where number 24 had stood was an inferno of flaming timbers and shattered walls.

Mrs Williams stood dumbstruck and stared. Then she began to scream. Little Tommy looked up in bewilderment.

"You look to Tommy, Jimmy," said Mum hastily. "Give 'im a slice of that bread."

Jimmy pulled the brown bag out from under his arm. He'd sat in that shelter throughout the raid with it squashed tightly under his arm and forgotten it. He emptied the crushed slices out on to the doorstep.

"One fer you, Tommy," he said, "an' one fer me."

Tommy stared wide-eyed at Jimmy and solemnly took the bread. Jimmy left his – he didn't feel like eating.

From round the corner came an ambulance, its siren ringing. It couldn't get along the street for the fallen rubble. A man in uniform jumped down and ran up.

"Anyone still in that house," he called briskly.

"No," said Mum. "Her husband's bin called away. The wife's all right, she's in with me."

"That's one less to worry about, thank God," called the ambulance man as he ran back. "I can hardly fit another one in the back."

A horn hooted continuously as a black taxicab came round the corner, crammed full of men in dark uniforms, trailing incongruously behind it what looked like a tank and pump on wheels. The cab doors burst open and four men from the Auxiliary Fire Service, in black jackets and helmets, leapt out and unwound the hoses.

"There's fires all over," one fire fighter gasped to George Munro as they aimed the spray at number 24. "We've gotta make do with taxicabs for the pumps."

A day ago Jimmy would have laughed at a taxi for a fire engine. It was strange what a difference a few hours made. Now he watched them anxiously, willing them to hurry.

Jimmy followed with Tommy as Mum led Mrs Williams inside and put the kettle on.

"They didn't get the gas main, so I suppose that's somethin'," smiled Mum.

Mrs Williams didn't seem to hear. She stared straight ahead.

Jimmy wanted to get back into the street to examine the damage, but Mrs Williams and Tommy stayed the rest of the evening. Jimmy didn't dare complain.

"Jimmy – put that kid in bed, there's a good lad."

Jimmy carried Tommy to his room. Tommy was a small child and didn't weigh much, but Jimmy's arms seemed weak and Tommy heavy. He pulled Tommy's boots off. The little boy was asleep before he got the last boot off.

Jimmy had to wake Tommy when the second raid came. Mum took Mrs Williams, and Jimmy carried the sleeping Tommy over his shoulder to the shelter. As they hurried down the street they could see flames from the fires of the afternoon, still burning, lighting up the night sky.

"Those fires," gasped George Munro as he pushed his tearful mother in front of him, "they're like signals they are. The Jerries 'ave only got to drop the bombs where they see the fires and they can bomb in the dark, like."

Wave after wave of bombers droned overhead. In the shelter Jimmy tried to lock his knees into a rigid position. If he let them shake they might sink beneath him. Around him people stood in silence now, staring with fixed eyes at the ceiling, listening to the battle going on outside.

At the all-clear they stumbled out into choking brick dust and smoke and a night sky lit up with an eerie orange glow. Over everything hung the bitter smell of smoke and burning.

Jimmy carried Tommy back home again. He pulled back the blankets on his bed and shoved the little boy in. Then he kicked off his shoes and squeezed in beside him. He hadn't done much but wait around and carry Tommy with him, but he was exhausted.

Jimmy woke to a hammering on the door. Something was sticking in his face. He'd forgotten about Tommy, whose feet were now threatening to gouge his eyes out. The little boy had wriggled right across the bed.

"Is Jimmy in, Mrs Smith?" Bob's voice rang up the stairs.

"I don't think he's awake. We was in the shelter most of last night."

Jimmy leapt out of bed, tugging his clothes off the chair.

"I'm coming'. Hold on, Bob!"

Mum gave them both a piece of bread and marge for breakfast. Bob ate ravenously.

"You had breakfast?" said Jimmy.

"Course not. I wanted to see the damage. You should see our street."

"Did yer Mum let you out?"

"She don't know. Got the little ones to look after, she 'as."

Outside the flames had gone. Number 24 was still smoking but the road in front was awash with mud and ash. Bob and Jimmy climbed over the rubble on the street to have a look.

"Look!" shouted Bob as he darted down to pick up a piece of sharp metal. "What d'you make of this?"

Jimmy carefully turned over the tiny piece of twisted, blackened metal and whistled.

"It's shrapnel . . . I bet it's shrapnel – from a German bomb."

They both stared at it in awe.

"Finders keepers!" said Bob and snatched it out of Jimmy's hand. He stuck it in his trouser pocket.

They were searching for more when they were chased off by a warden.

"Get off! You'll get killed if this lot falls on you."

Then they met up with the rest of the gang and tried to go and look at the damage to the engine sheds. They wriggled under the fence, but were spotted and chased out. They tried it several times. It was a wonderful morning, climbing the fallen timber and collapsed walls, finding old entries blocked and new pathways opened up. Yesterday was a forgotten nightmare, but today – Jimmy wished today would go on for ever.

"Meet you after dinner then," said Jimmy to Bob.

"Can't. I'm off this afternoon."

"Off?"

"Bein' evacuated, me and me sisters, to Devon."

They stared at each other.

"You's goin' to Canada soon, ain't you?"

Jimmy nodded. He didn't dare speak. He and Bob had been together since the first class at Infant School, that was eight years ago. Jimmy couldn't imagine life without Bob.

"Right," said Bob. "Best be off, or me mum will blow me top off worse than the Jerries."

They both tried to grin, but they couldn't.

"Look after me shrapnel then." Bob delved in his pocket and shoved the twisted metal at Jimmy.

"Don't you want it?"

"I can get some more . . . They won't have bombs in Canada."

22

"Thanks!"

Jimmy walked home. Life was changing, he knew it. He hoped he got to Canada quick.

The bombers came back on Sunday and Dad was still away.

People shouted at each other in the warehouse cellar and pushed and shoved. It was too small for everyone trying to get in. Old Mrs Munro refused to budge from upstairs and said she'd rather die in her bed than die from her bad joints in the shelter.

Jimmy's mother sat bolt upright with her arm round Jimmy's shoulder. When the droning of the bombers came, her hand tightened and gripped his shoulder, and when the explosions burst out he could hear her suck in her breath, and feel her rigid back beside him. She never said anything, never cried out as some people did, but he knew she was frightened too.

There were the same screams and crying when they emerged from the cellar to the flickering orange light of the fires.

Their house was untouched but the glass in the front door was cracked. Jimmy helped Mum tape the cracked glass.

"We'd best do them all," she said.

Jimmy spent the rest of Sunday sticking tape over the windows in criss-cross patterns, trying not to think of Bob.

That evening Dad came home, exhausted and grimy with smoke and coaldust from the engines.

"Bob gone then, has he? You should be hearin' soon too, Jimmy."

"I can't go, Dad."

"Not go, Jimmy? I know you don't want to leave us, son, but it's fer the best. Yer mother and me have made up our minds on that one."

"I'm stoppin'." The words squeezed out agonisingly.

"No you ain't, son."

Mum set down her iron and stared at Jimmy.

"I heard you tellin' Bob you couldn't wait to go." She regarded him quizzically.

"Well . . . I've changed me mind."

"What 'ud the world be like if we all changed our minds every day," said his father. He looked tired and angry. "You'll do as yer told."

Jimmy felt his mother's hand land on his head.

"It's not me yer worried about, is it, Jimmy? You mustn't think about it. I'll be just fine."

"But Dad's never here. You hate the bombin', the warehouse."

"People's frightened, Jimmy. That's why they shout at each other. We'll get used to it and it'll calm down."

His father's face relaxed in a smile.

"Don't you worry, Jim. If there's a raid later, we're goin' down the tube station. They're unlockin' the doors tonight. There's acres of platform down there and space to sleep an' all. We'll be out of earshot under ground."

That night, at the first wail of the siren, Dad rushed them all along Union Street, round into Middle Lane, and down the underground entrance next to the green-grocer's. There was a queue all down the stairs, but it was worth it. The long platform was like a palace. Each family had marked out its little area and brought blankets to sleep on, and the platform was covered with an untidy jumble of bodies.

Some ladies in uniform organised a singsong, and for the first time for three days Jimmy had something like a long sleep with his mother sleeping beside him, and he didn't wake up until the first train rattled into the station in the morning.

When they got home and opened the door, a buff envelope lay on the mat with the letters CORB in black lettering along the top. Jimmy's father picked it up.

"Yer goin' Wednesday, son. Got to get you to Liverpool," his father said with relief.

He was going! He couldn't believe it.

Jimmy and his father avoided looking at his mother.

Mum went into the kitchen and they heard the gas ring hissing.

"Cup of tea anyone?" came her calm voice.

Dad smiled encouragingly at Jimmy.

" 'Fraid it mebbe goodbye, son. I'm drivin' again tonight and I don't know if I'll be back before

Wednesday." He paused. "Jimmy, don't say a word to yer mother, but if you takes a fancy to Canada, don't come back. There's a whole new world out there. When this war's over, we'll come and join you."

"They need engine drivers, Dad," said Jimmy happily. "The track there goes for hundreds and hundreds of miles . . ."

"Is that a fact?" said his father, and together they went into the kitchen.

Wednesday was a grey, chill day. Jimmy's mother dressed in her best clothes, the black coat she had got for the first funeral and which had done the other three, and which made her look serious and important. She'd even got on her black felt hat and a pair of nylon stockings. Mum hadn't worn stockings since the war started. She was white-faced, but Jimmy was proud of her.

"You got yer label on, Jimmy?"

"It's round me neck." Jimmy waved the luggage label on its string with his name on.

"Don't forget yer bag when the train gets to Liverpool."

"I won't."

"You got yer sandwiches?"

"In me pocket."

"Don't forget to send a card from Liverpool."

"Shouldn't think there'll be time."

"One from Canada then."

Jimmy shifted uneasily from foot to foot on the long station platform. Mum was trying hard to put a good face on it, but he wished he could get away soon. Seeing her struggling upset him too. As they chatted about nothing, the platform filled up with other boys and girls.

A young man with brown-rimmed glasses, who peered like a clever owl at a list in his hands, came up.

"James Smith?" He checked Jimmy's label.

"Yes."

"In carriage number five."

Jimmy was in the carriage, waving out of the window, when his father came running down the platform. He was in coal-grimed dungarees and his face was smeared with coal-dust.

"Thought I might make it!" he yelled and smiled. "Here, son, take this."

Jimmy reached down to take the coins held up in his father's hand.

"Thanks, Dad!"

Jimmy had never had pocket money in his life before. Dad would have to do without. Perhaps he ought to give it to Mum . . .

"Bye, Jimmy."

The train had started to creak as the couplings moved forward. Dad waved and put his arm round Mum. She stood still and straight, and then blew him a kiss. Then they both waved, disappearing in a cloud of steam as the train puffed away.

Jimmy sank back in his seat, examined the coins and put them in his pocket. It was really happening! If only he had Bob with him it would be perfect.

Opposite sat a girl about his age. She had a mass of curly red hair. Beside her sat a smaller girl, with the same red curls, clutching a large, new-looking china doll. The little girl's face was streaked with tears and she looked at Jimmy fearfully. Jimmy smiled at her. She reminded him of his sister.

The little girl just stared, but her sister said in a friendly fashion. "What's yer name then?"

"Jimmy Smith."

"I'm Pat Banks and this is me little sister Jean. We're sailin' on Friday."

"What are we sailin' in?" asked a boy a year or so younger than Jimmy. He had thin legs that stuck out from his short trousers like matchsticks, and thin lanky hair to match. Beside him sat another little girl with the same stick-thin legs, but a scaled-down version of the boy. She wriggled around and fidgeted with a little purse she was carrying.

"I've got pocket money as well," she announced proudly.

"No need to show off, Babs," said her brother.

The little girl pulled a face and they all laughed.

Huddled up in the corner, a handsome boy with dark brown hair, which shone as Dad's did when he put hair cream on for special nights out, stared at them all, scowling.

28

"What's yer name, then?" asked Jimmy as the dark brown eyes surveyed him.

The boy uncrossed a pair of long, strong legs, folded arms that were far too long for his tight jacket and ignored Jimmy. Jimmy could see the boy's jutting chin and shiny hair reflected in the window. His own reflection hovered to one side of it, with his plump face and wiry hair. He was glad he'd got a bit thinner since rationing had come in.

Then, as they sat waiting to hear, the boy turned.

"I don't talk to sissies."

Jimmy sat there stunned.

"Yer not very nice, I must say," said Pat.

The boy ignored her. Then he turned to Jimmy with a smile on his face.

"D'you remember to kiss Mumsie, then? Mummy's sweetie-pie, 'ent you?"

The silence in the carriage was icy. The chatting stopped.

CHAPTER THREE

The journey wasn't much fun. The boy with match-stick legs was called Sidney and he shared his *Beano* with Jimmy. The dark, handsome boy looked on disdainfully. Jimmy wasn't going to risk another conversation with him, so he read and re-read the *Beano* and fingered Bob's bit of shrapnel in his pocket.

At Liverpool they stumbled out of the train, dragging their suitcases with them. The station didn't look much different from the station they'd left, but the voices around Jimmy were different. Nobody spoke like they did at home. It was a funny way of speaking. But people smiled as they saw the tired, wan-faced children tumbling out. In London people had looked annoyed with all the evacuee children blocking the platform.

"Where are you going then, luv?" asked a lady in a man's ancient raincoat, bending over Babs.

"To . . . to . . ." Babs tried to speak but her face began to crumple.

"To Canada," explained Sidney quickly.

"Canada? Why, that's grand! I don't mind a holiday in Canada meself. Will you take me with you, luv?"

Babs face softened and she grinned.

They were taken in a green bus through streets of

grimy brick houses, past blackened stone buildings surrounded by mounds of sandbags. Overhead a huge barrage balloon floated. Jimmy tried to get away from the dark-haired boy and sat at the front of the bus with Sidney and his little sister, Babs. To his relief the dark-haired boy went down to the back and sat on his own.

The bus stopped in front of a tall brick building where children clutching suitcases and gas masks stood in a line up to the door.

A young man, tanned and fit-looking, who smiled with teeth as white as his open-necked sports shirt, bounded on to the bus.

"Welcome to Mountford Children's Home!" he announced. "Girls check with me and turn to the left outside the bus, boys to the right. And, oh – don't forget your gas masks."

Jimmy slung his gas mask over his shoulder and followed Sidney and Babs off the bus.

"Barbara Wilks, please, mister," Babs whispered to the young man with the list.

"Jolly good, Barbara! Careful down the steps now."

The young man put a tick on the list in his hand.

"Sidney Wilks, if you please, mister."

"To the right, Sidney."

"Mister?"

"Yes, Sidney?"

"Children's 'ome? Was you meanin' an orphanage, mister? Babs and me, we ain't no orphans, mister . . ."

"Good Lord no!" exclaimed the cheerful young

man, swiping some blond strands of hair back from his face as he chuckled out loud. "Don't you worry, Sidney. This *was* an orphanage, but the children have been evacuated to the country. We're borrowing it until you board ship. Now, let's hand your little sister over to Miss Partridge here."

Bab's bottom lip quivered.

"Go on, Babs," said Sidney. "I'll see you later, at tea – won't I mister?"

"Rather!" said the young man. With his hand he shoved back a few more unruly strands of hair and put a tick beside the next child on his list.

"I'll take her with us," said Pat, the friendly girl from the train.

"That's the way!" said the young man with a smiling dazzle of white teeth.

Pat looked a bit white-faced herself but she followed Miss Partridge with little Jean and her doll on one hand, and Babs on the other.

Jimmy felt sick in his stomach too. He didn't know anyone. He never thought he'd miss a familiar face so much. He clutched his gas mask in one hand and his bag in the other, and followed the line of boys into the house. He glanced back and saw the boy with dark hair at the back of the line. At least he'd got away from him.

They were told to lay all their belongings out on a table for a stout lady in green uniform to check over.

"We can't have the Canadians thinking our children

aren't clothed decently," she said firmly to the boy in front of Jimmy as his battered old boots, bursting at the back, were thrown into a bin and replaced with a new pair of shiny, black shoes.

Jimmy's clothes passed muster.

"Here's one to be proud of his mother!" exclaimed the lady in a deep voice that made Jimmy jump. She examined his clothes, all mended, cleaned and ironed by his mother, and smiled grimly.

He stuffed the clothes back in his suitcase and kept his head down. His mum . . . It was daft really, but he missed her already.

The dark-haired boy was kept ages by the stout lady. Clothes were carried in and out and he emerged with a brand-new suitcase.

Then they all queued again in their underclothes for the doctor to look at them.

The stethoscope pressed coldly against Jimmy's chest.

"At last a child who has been adequately fed!" a worried-looking doctor in gold-rimmed spectacles said to the nurse beside him. He tapped Jimmy's chest and nodded. It reminded Jimmy of looking over the grey-hounds at the dog track.

Sidney, with the lanky legs, was kept in for ages.

"Thought they 'ud never let me alone," he whispered to Jimmy as he put his clothes back on.

Jimmy looked at his skinny arms and his sharp shoulder blades. "Why?"

"They thought I 'ad TB or somethin'."

"You OK, then?"

"Course I am." And Sidney gave Jimmy a quick punch in the ribs.

Jimmy swung a blow to Sidney's arm, taking care not to bash him too hard. He wasn't convinced – Sidney didn't look as if he could take much bashing.

"Good gracious, fighting already, boys!" called a deep, disapproving voice.

The stout lady in uniform, who had inspected their clothes, bore down on them, her arms laden with boxes.

"We was playin', missus," Jimmy explained.

"It looked awfully like fighting to me. You'd better come and stand over here, both of you."

The boy with dark hair was waiting in the corner too.

"How's Mumsie?" he hissed and kicked Jimmy in the ankle.

"Ow!"

"Still fighting," bellowed the stout lady as she put down a box marked 'socks'. "We're certainly not sending hooligans to Canada! So, if you want to go, we shall need a better class of behaviour."

Her smile had vanished and she gave Jimmy a long, meaningful stare, as if it was all his fault.

That night they slept in the cellars on mattresses laid out on the floor. The mattresses were pushed up tight together and Jimmy managed to get in between the

34

spindly Sidney and a boy in glasses who had just arrived from Southampton.

Jimmy and Sidney had a game of snap, while the boy from Southampton watched and looked at a book from time to time.

"You brought that book with you?" asked Sidney.

"Yes – it's got a lot of information about Canada in it. It's a gazetteer of the North American continent."

Sidney stared at Jimmy, but Jimmy didn't know what the boy was going on about. He tried to avoid Sidney's stare and look knowledgeable.

"Who gave you that then?" said Sidney lamely.

The boy's face quivered. "It was my father's."

"And he let you take it!" Jimmy exclaimed. "We've only got a Bible in our home, and it has to stay on the sideboard. My mum says you don't need no other books with a Bible in the home. I bet your dad don't know you got it!"

"He's dead. My parents died two nights ago when the house was bombed and I don't want to talk about it, if you don't mind."

The boy took his glasses off, blew on them and rubbed them hard on his sleeve.

Jimmy and Sidney looked at each other. They were bursting with questions but the boy had turned away on his side.

"I'm Jimmy and he's Sidney," said Jimmy. "What's yer name?"

The boy turned back. "Keith," he said.

Both parents dead! Jimmy couldn't imagine a life with no Mum and Dad. He wasn't going to see them for a while but he knew they were there, waiting for him at home, when the war would be finished. If they were bombed and killed . . . It was too terrible to imagine . . . And this boy Keith . . .

"Want to see me piece of German shrapnel, Keith?" said Jimmy, and he laid the bit of twisted metal on the bed for both boys to see.

That night the sirens went.

Jimmy hadn't realised the Germans had got as far as Liverpool.

"Course they 'ave," said Sidney. "They bomb the docks to stop food and supplies gettin' in and out from America and Canada, me dad says. You should know that, Keith, because you got the navy down South-ampton way, ent you?"

Jimmy and Sidney were sitting up in bed listening to the wailing.

Keith didn't answer. He was a mound under the blankets.

Jimmy put his hand across. The blankets were shaking. He lifted a corner.

"Don't you worry, Keith. I've got me hand on the shrapnel. It's lucky it is. Germans don't bomb their own shrapnel, do they, Sidney?"

"Well, I don't rightly . . ."

"Well they don't!" Jimmy said firmly.

The following day they met the escorts who were going to accompany them to Canada. Jimmy was pleased to find himself in a group with Sidney, Keith and three other boys. The boy with dark hair was in a different group with a pale-faced clergyman as escort.

Jimmy's escort was the jolly young man with the white teeth, who had checked them in when they arrived. He was called Mr Barry. He was going to be a clergyman too one day, but at the moment he had volunteered to help with the evacuation. His hobby was motor racing and he showed them a photograph of a round dark beetle of a car that he said he had built himself.

Jimmy couldn't believe his luck, to have landed an escort who raced cars! He couldn't wait to tell Dad.

The younger escorts, like Mr Barry, organised games for the boys. Jimmy liked football but he wasn't brilliant at it. Once he managed to get the ball and he was panting towards the goal when the tall, dark-haired boy came from nowhere, shoved him aside and took over the ball. It didn't make sense as they were both on the same side.

The dark-haired boy scored.

"Why d'ya do that?" shouted Jimmy angrily. "It was my ball."

"You wouldna' made it, fattie," called the boy, tossing his sleek hair out of his eyes.

The boys around them laughed. Jimmy felt his cheeks blaze. The game wasn't the same after that.

The next night there was a fiercer raid. The explosions were louder and even the blackouts over the high windows could not blot out the flickering of the fires. The escorts whispered together. Keith leapt up and tried to run out and had to be dragged back by Mr Barry.

"The sooner we get these children to Canada the better," Jimmy heard the clergyman whisper to Mr Barry. "There are some that can't take any more bombing . . . they're too disturbed already."

The next morning, Friday, they were loaded on to two green buses, ninety children in all, and their suitcases checked and stacked in the boot.

Jimmy got on the bus and kept a seat for Sidney, who had gone off to check that Babs was safely on the girls' bus. The dark-haired boy appeared at the top of the bus steps and surveyed the seats. Jimmy pretended to be looking at something outside the window but he heard the boy stamp along and stop by his seat.

"I'm keepin' a place for me friend." Jimmy tried to sounded casual.

"You only met him Wednesday. He's not yer friend."

The boy slumped in the seat beside Jimmy.

"It's for Sidney!" Jimmy protested.

"Come along, Jimmy," Mr Barry's face loomed up. "Don't be unfriendly. Everyone sits where they want – make room for George here."

"Cissies don't have friends." George laughed in Jimmy's face when Mr Barry had gone. "Specially fat cissies."

It was a relief to shake George off at the docks. Jimmy ran over to Sidney and Keith.

"You said you 'ud keep me a seat!" exclaimed Sidney.

"I did. That big lad with the dark hair, he's called George, he took it."

"We could do without 'im!"

The three boys looked around them in amazement. The docks were full of ships of all sizes. There were tankers stacked up two or three deep against the dock, squat tugs puffing black smoke out of their funnels as they manoeuvred, freighters with their hatches open as a forest of cranes lifted out bulging sacks in huge rope nets. There was the creaking of the cranes, the puffing of the railway running through the docks, the shouts of men swarming in and out of huge dirty brick warehouses, the hooting of boat sirens, and above it all the relentless roar of the wind.

And towering over everything at the dockside was the most beautiful ocean-going liner. Jimmy had seen pictures of liners before, but he hadn't been able to imagine their size from a picture. Its grey hull rose up sheer beside them, so high that the edge of the deck railings was way above them. It was far bigger than he had expected.

". . . camouflage; you see."

"What you goin' on about, Keith?" Jimmy had only been half-listening.

"I told you," Keith shouted in his ear. "They're painting all the civilian ships grey or buff now. I bet it was snow-white before the war. It's camouflage – so they can't be seen so easily out at sea."

The boys moved back to get a better look. The funnels sloped back in an elegant line, and at either end of the ship were two sloping masts, tapering to a point at their tips. From the masts, colourful triangular flags flapped and fluttered against a backdrop of grey sky and scudding, charcoal-grey clouds. Grey or not, it was still a beautiful ship.

Sidney nudged Jimmy.

"It's all right, ent it?" he laughed, and Jimmy grinned back. Yes – it was more than all right!

"It's not an 'it'," said Keith. "Ships are always 'she'."

"She's all right," agreed Jimmy.

The ship was a hive of action. Brown-skinned men in white uniforms rushed up and down the gangplanks, carrying passengers' luggage into the liner. A group of sailors in the dark blue uniform of the Royal Navy laughed and chatted, or waved to wives and girlfriends below as they carried their kitbags on board. Overhead, cranes rattled and screeched as they lifted stores sky-high above the ship and lowered them gingerly to the deck hands below. So much bustle and noise! Jimmy laughed with sheer excitement. This was what he had been waiting for!

Mr Barry lined the boys up and they filed up a gangplank.

"Look at those ropes, Sidney," said Jimmy, pointing to the heavy ropes that moored the ship to round pillars on the quay. "Thick as me dad's arm."

The white life belts fastened at intervals to the rails stood out like washing on a line to dry against the ship's grey paint. *City of Karachi*, the black writing on them said.

"*City of Karachi* . . . That's the name of the ship, Sidney. Eh, Keith, where's Karachi then?"

"The Indian sub-continent," said Keith.

"That don't sound right for a Liverpool ship," said Sidney.

"I expect she usually sails the India run," said Keith. "Her crew look like Lascars. They've called in every ship they can for the convoys to America, and we still haven't got enough."

It was all right having Keith around – he knew an awful lot of interesting stuff.

"Well they ain't goin' to need a lot more ships if they've got ones like the *City of Karachi*," said Sidney proudly. "I reckon we got the best!"

"Where are my boys? Jimmy! Sidney! Keith! There you are!" said Mr Barry. With fair hair blowing across his wind-reddened face, he was grinning as much as they were. He tugged along the other three boys in their group behind him. "Righty ho! Follow me."

Mr Barry led them up the gangplank and along the

deck. Deck chairs were stacked behind a rope and huge lifeboats were suspended from winches above their heads. They followed a lady in a fur coat with a girl of about Jimmy's age. The girl was in a green coat with a green velvet collar and matching velvet beret, which she had to hold on to because of the wind. Jimmy felt a nudge in his back and turned to catch Sidney's grin. He couldn't see Madge or Doreen dressed up like that. The mother and daughter turned off through a door marked with black lettering FIRST CLASS PASSENGERS ONLY.

They went down some metal stairs to another level, below deck, SECOND CLASS PASSENGER AREA, and then on down yet steeper stairs following arrows that led to CABIN CLASS.

"We're in the stern – the back of the ship," said Mr Barry. "Girls one side and boys the other."

Jimmy, Sidney and Keith managed to get a cabin together. It was a tiny room with a porthole just above sea level. Two bunks with grey blankets, set one above the other, were on the inside wall, and one below the porthole window. There was a small basin, with its own tap, and cupboards cleverly fitted under the bunks. They decided they would take it in turns on the porthole bunk and Jimmy could start as he had the lucky shrapnel.

"'Ere! Come and look at this." Sidney had slipped outside the cabin to explore.

"Where are you, Sid?"

"In 'ere."

Jimmy pushed open the door of the room opposite theirs. Sidney was standing staring, a look of horror on his face.

"What do you reckon this place is?"

Jimmy stared at the gleaming white tiles and shivered. It looked a bit like the butcher's shop in Union Street.

"It's a bathroom," said Keith.

Jimmy stared at the gaping white bath. They had a tin tub at home. Mum lifted it down off the wall every Saturday night. She had to heat pans of water on the range, then she had first bath, Jimmy second and Dad last as he was the dirtiest with all the coal grime from the engines.

"I'll not need this," he said with relief. "Mum got the bath down special, the night before I came. I could be in Canada before next Saturday."

"Me too," said Sidney anxiously. He had begun to fiddle with the big metal taps at the end of the bath. Water came spouting out, with clouds of steam rising as the bath filled.

"Blimey," he said, "it's hot this – 'ere, you feel, Jimmy." He turned the tap off and tried the other one. Cold water came gushing from it.

"Bet it's sea water," said Jimmy.

He put his finger under the tap and licked it. The water tasted all right; it wasn't salty. He pressed his hand up against the tap. A great spray of water sprang out sideways across the room, showering Sidney's face.

Sidney gulped as the water flattened his lanky hair

even more, then he grinned. "I might have a bath and all!"

Down the corridor they heard Mr Barry's voice calling. The boys backed guiltily to the door, across the white tiles muddied by their wet shoes. At the door, leaning against the doorpost, was George. He must have been watching them all the time. He vanished.

"Come up, boys," bellowed Mr Barry. "Come and look – we're casting off!"

They peered over the railings on deck, watching the small black tugs nudge and pull the great liner from her berth. Black smoke was pouring from her funnels and from the funnels of the little tugs. The wind was blowing the smoke all in one direction, out into the wide river, like so many black streamers. The tugs pulled the ship away from the quay, away from the fluttering white handkerchiefs in the hands of the families and friends standing on the dock. Jimmy wished Mum and Dad were there too.

The tugs pulled the ship out into the river – the Mersey Mr Barry called it – and guided the ship on and out towards the sea. Jimmy could still hear the shouting on the dock walls, borne towards them on the wind. The liner belched out three great hoots as she edged away, and all along the quayside people stood waving.

"Best of luck!" a voice shouted.

Luck . . . Did they need luck? Good thing he'd got Bob's shrapnel then, and he fingered it in his pocket.

Slowly they edged past the lines of ships and cranes and towering dark warehouses, out into mid-stream.

"Look," said Jimmy. "That building. It's fallin' down – it's bombed, it is."

They stared at the burnt shell of a warehouse, festooned with charred boxes hanging from suspended floors. Next to it was what must once have been a timber yard. Planks of wood, reduced to charcoal, still stood in places.

The boys gazed silently.

"Well, we heard the bombs, didn't we?" said Sidney at last.

Suddenly Jimmy knew he couldn't wait to get out on the open sea.

The big ship edged down the river. At its mouth a veritable fleet of cargo ships, tankers and freighters was waiting for them. Jimmy tried to count them and he reckoned there could be twenty to thirty ships in all.

"They waitin' for us, mister?" Jimmy nudged Mr Barry on the arm.

"Yes, Jimmy. We've got the commodore of the convoy aboard the *Karachi*. Ours is the biggest ship – we'll probably take centre position."

"Look at that, Jimmy – a destroyer!" shouted Sidney.

Jimmy looked in the direction of his pointing finger. Approaching at speed was a grey destroyer. It looked surprisingly small in comparison with the *Karachi*. Its sleek lines bristled with gun emplacements, two towers of gun turrets, one above each other, on the front deck, steaming into view. Behind the destroyer followed two smaller gunships.

"Those," said Keith, peering through his glasses, "are corvettes. I've seen one in Southampton. They're new, to protect the convoys."

"A little ship like that can't do much," said Jimmy doubtfully as he stared out at all the shipping it would have to protect.

"Yes it can. It drops depth charges to stop enemy submarines."

Jimmy and Sidney stared at Keith, amazed at his knowledge. They were both silent. German submarines, going underneath them?

Jimmy glanced up at the first-class decks and funnels towering above them. Their ship was the biggest there.

"I reckon we're big enough."

"Course we are," agreed Sidney, peering down over the rails. "Biggest of the lot, we are. Nothin' could touch us."

Keith opened his mouth, but he caught Jimmy's eye and shut it again.

Mr Barry handed them out life jackets, fatly stuffed with something that felt like a heavy cushion. He showed them how to tie the two strings on the front in tight bows. "Now you're to keep these on at all times."

"Where do we put them when we're in our bunks, mister?" Sidney asked.

"Never take them off. You sleep in them over your pyjamas." He checked their strings. "Now have I made myself quite clear? You wear them night and day. Never let me catch you without one!"

That evening the boys filed into the dining room in their life jackets. Jimmy stared, open-mouthed. He'd never seen a room like it. It was all cream pillars and soft wall lights and tables draped with white tablecloths. There were white bits of linen moulded into funny fan shapes in front of each place and rows of polished forks and knives and spoons by each plate.

Round the walls stood dark-skinned men, proud and elegant in white, high-buttoned uniforms with wide blue sashes and wearing white gloves. Gloves in a dining room!

At the far end of the room were smaller, round tables. Jimmy caught sight of the girl he'd seen earlier. Her green coat was gone and she was dressed all in pink, with her brown hair falling in ringlets and with a matching pink bow in her hair.

At their end of the dining room stood a long row of tables. Jimmy glimpsed the tossing red curls of Pat and little Jean. Sidney asked if Babs could sit with him, and her escort, a pretty young woman, with friendly blue eyes said she could. Babs sat there as quiet as a mouse, her eyes fixed in awe on the table-cloth in front of her.

On the table, in a shiny, silver holder, was a printed

47

card. Jimmy got the shock of his life when one of the smart waiters tapped him on the shoulder and pointed to the card with a white-gloved finger.

Menu, it said. It seemed to be a list of food.

Jimmy held the card while Keith and Sidney leant across either side to have a look.

MENU
Fish Puffs
Chestnut Soup
Oeufs Mornay

Fish and Leek Pudding
Game Pie
Pancake Alexandre

Sultana and Toffee Pudding
Victory Sponge
Prune Jelly

"Blimey!" said Jimmy. "Sounds all right."

Sidney hissed out a low whistle. Mr Barry looked down towards them to see where the whistle had come from, but all three ducked their heads down.

The brown-skinned man in the white jacket stood beside them with a pencil and pad in his hand, waiting.

"I think he wants us to say something," whispered Keith, looking over his shoulder.

"Very nice too," said Jimmy. "We'll 'ave it."

The man pointed at the menu again.

"Lovely," said Sidney politely. "I'll 'ave it too."

"Me too," said Keith, uncertainly.

The man smiled and wrote.

CHAPTER FOUR

Jimmy was woken by a bell hammering away behind his head. For a moment he couldn't think where he was. His stomach felt sick and heavy, and his bed was heaving from side to side. He was about to yell "Mum!", when he felt the high edges of the wooden bunk and remembered.

He turned over and watched the hammer beating away on the little bell above the cabin door.

"Hey, Sidney, Keith! It's the drill bell."

Keith sat up shaking, burrowed around under his pillow and pulled out his spectacles. He blew on them, cleaned them with the edge of his pyjama jacket and set them on his nose.

"Drill – right! We'd better get dressed then."

A groan came from the top bunk as Sidney's wispy hair appeared.

"You OK, Sidney?" asked Jimmy anxiously. The noise didn't sound too good.

Sidney's face peered over the edge of the bunk. He'd never looked too healthy but now, with his yellow face and pale lips, he certainly looked ill.

"You stay in bed, Sidney," said Jimmy. "I'll tell Mr Barry you ain't too good."

Sidney swung his stick legs over the edge.

"Course I'm comin'. Nothin' wrong with me," he muttered grimly. "Just that Victory Sponge didn't do nothin' for the Prune Jelly," he added.

They were slowly pulling on their clothes when the door burst open. Mr Barry stood on the threshold. The blond strands of hair fell over a furrowed and frowning brow and his mouth was set in a tight line.

"What *do* you think you're doing?" he exploded.

They looked at him in amazement, astonished at his changed manner.

"This is meant to be an emergency practice. Why aren't your clothes on? Why do you think I told you to wear your life jackets at all times?"

"We was," said Jimmy indignantly. "They was over the pyjamas, like you said. But I can't get me clothes on, if I don't take me life jacket off first."

"Why aren't you in your clothes? You have to keep them on day and night while we're in the danger zone."

"You didn't tell us about no danger zone, mister," said Sidney. "You mean we gotta sleep in all our clothes?"

"Yes – yes. Didn't I tell you?" Mr Barry sounded exasperated. "Do you think the Germans are going to allow you time to get your clothes on. Get out of here, quick, to your boat station. Jimmy, did you hear me? Out! Now!"

"I'll just get me trousers on, mister."

"No you won't!"

Jimmy was in his underpants, Keith in his trousers with one sock on, while Sidney had only his vest and pyjama trousers on. They followed Mr Barry in an orderly file up the flight of stairs and around the deck to lifeboat station number 8.

"What's got into 'im?" whispered Sidney.

Jimmy shrugged. He hoped Mr Barry wasn't going to be like some schoolmasters he'd come across – all smiles and laughs in front of the other teachers, but like demons once the classroom door was shut.

He kept in close behind Keith. There was a strong wind blowing and his bare legs were freezing. They followed in single file round the rolling deck to a lifeboat suspended above them by pulleys and marked with the figure 8. It looked like one of the bigger boats. Other groups of children were already there with their escorts, but Mr Barry was in overall charge.

"I'm not having this muddle again," he shouted, bellowing above the roar of the wind. "We've made it this time – but too late! Now, let's learn from this. As soon as you hear the bells, you drop what you're doing, walk in an orderly line, out to station number 8. Any questions?"

Sidney put up his hand.

"Mister – my sister, Babs? She's got to be here with me. My mum said I've got to look after her."

"We can't worry about Babs," snapped Mr Barry. "The girls are with their escorts and Babs is, I'm sure, happy with the younger children and looked after better than you or I ever could. That reminds me – Sidney, Jimmy, Keith, go gently now on breakfast. You choose *one* cooked dish off the menu, not the lot, *one* dish from each section, do you understand?"

Jimmy stared at Sidney with relief. He knew if he'd gone on eating like last night he'd have burst like a balloon. One dish off each section . . .

"Hey! What do you think they do with the rest?" whispered Sidney. "Chuck it in the bin?"

"I expect it's planned," said Keith. "If some people choose one dish, other people will make different choices so there shouldn't be much waste."

Jimmy nodded. Keith could think all right, there was no doubt about that.

"Fatty! Pink legs! Bit of piggy with crackling on top, ain't 'e."

The giggling and laughter were coming from in front of them. Jimmy shivered as he recognised the voice.

"Don't listen," said Sidney. "If they want trouble we'll do 'em in."

Watching Sidney's skinny frame, with his stick legs in their flapping pyjama trousers, marching back to the cabin in front of him, Jimmy didn't believe him. The taunts seemed to have come out of the lifeboat they were walking under. George must have climbed up into the boat, something that was strictly forbidden.

George wasn't alone. He was waiting in the passage at the door to their cabin, leaning against the door and blocking the way in. Two younger boys were with him, tough freckle-faced lads, one with a broken front tooth.

"You get in when you've paid the fare," the boy with the broken tooth grinned.

"What do you mean?" said Keith indignantly.

"Give us a penny each one, that's three pennies from each of you, and we'll leave yer alone."

Jimmy, Sidney and Keith stared at each other. Jimmy and Sidney had precious pocket money for the first time in their lives. Keith hadn't got any because of his parents being dead, so Jimmy had persuaded Sidney that it would be fair if they each gave a third of their money to Keith. Sidney had taken some persuading, so Jimmy had taken him into the passage so that Keith wouldn't hear. George must have heard them.

The colour rose on Sidney's scrawny neck. He plunged forward at the broken-toothed boy. Sidney was thrown back against the wall, like a fly being swatted, just as Mr Barry came down the steps.

"I've had my fill of you lot! Come on and get to breakfast or you'll be going without."

George and his gang sauntered off smirking.

"Why's he picking on us?" said Keith. "He was all right yesterday."

"You OK, Sidney?" asked Jimmy.

"I'll murder that George if 'e comes near us again," said Sidney, rubbing his elbow. "I really will."

★

Babs came to see Sidney in the games room after breakfast. She was hand in hand with little Jean and carrying Jean's new doll.

"Nice doll!" said Sidney. "All right then, Babs?"

Babs ran off laughing with Jean, and Jimmy thought Sidney looked put out.

"Come on, Sidney. We'll play snakes and ladders next," said Jimmy.

The escorts kept them occupied with board games and ping pong, and sing-alongs. Keith sat by himself in a corner, hunched over a chessboard. One of the escorts went up to him from time to time and moved a figure on the board.

Jimmy glanced up from the snakes and ladders board. The cabin windows were streaked with running drops of water. It wasn't raining so it must have been from the spray. The ship was rolling so much he felt giddy when he stood up.

"I'm bored with this," he said to Sidney. "Let's get out there."

Sidney glanced at the windows. "We allowed to . . . ?" he began. "Let's go," he grinned."What about Keith?"

Keith looked up absent-mindedly as they told him what they were planning to do.

"Wait . . ." he said vaguely.

It was clear he wasn't listening. The game of chess had really got him. Jimmy bent down and tried to make head or tail of the black and white figures scattered around the squares.

The ship rolled, or was he pushed? Jimmy fell forward, shooting the pieces off the board.

"Clumsy!" yelled a sarcastic voice.

It was George, he knew, he didn't need to look.

"Sorry, Keith. I didn't mean to – the ship . . ."

Sidney was scrabbling on the floor picking up the pieces.

"We can put 'em back," he said hopefully.

"It's no good now," said Keith mournfully. "I can't remember where they all were."

"We're goin' on deck," said Jimmy. "All these games and singsongs is all right, but there's a right wind blowin' outside. Come with us."

The boys gripped the heaving wooden railing and stared out. On either side of the *Karachi*, stretching away to the horizon, were strings of ships, two or three ships set at wide intervals behind each other. They were like a shoal of whales swimming in parallel lines, two or three to a line, except they weren't swimming straight, sometimes steaming out to one side and then back to the other.

"They're making heavy weather of it," shouted Keith. "They're not steering in a straight line."

"Course they can't," yelled Jimmy. "Look at those waves. I couldn't swim straight in that lot, so I suppose they can't."

56

The *Karachi* was rolling enough, and it was the biggest ship in the convoy, tossed around on restless, foam-spattered dark waves. Ahead of them steamed the destroyer, the foam from huge waves breaking over its decks and swirling round its guns. For a moment it seemed as if it would go on down for ever but then up it rose on the next wave, with bows pointing up skyward.

"Crikey!" said Sidney.

The air felt cold and clean against Jimmy's cheek after the fug of the cabin. The wind, blowing in great gusts, roared in his ears and lifted the tufts on his head. Overhead the sky was a mass of scudding dark clouds.

"It ain't half rough," he said.

"What did you say?" shouted Keith in his ear.

"How many ships would there be?" yelled Jimmy.

"I've counted eighteen," said Keith. "There may be more hidden by waves."

"Look!" shouted Sidney.

A huge plane appeared out of the clouds overhead, its engine all but drowned by the howling wind. The Lascar sailors, coiling ropes on the deck, stopped and stared at the destroyer ahead. Jimmy turned back and looked up at the bridge behind them.

"What's he up to?" He nudged Sidney and Keith.

A man in Royal Navy uniform was watching the plane through binoculars. He said something to an older man wearing a uniform with a lot of gold bars on. They smiled and put the binoculars away.

57

"Bet they thought it was a German Focke-Wulf," said Keith." But it's a Sunderland – on escort duty, watching out for German submarines."

They waved at the plane and then leant forward staring at the expanse of the sea and sky before them.

". . . they're zig-zagging," a deep foreign voice drifted down on the wind, from the first-class deck above them: "Each ship zig-zags within its line. It makes it more difficult for a U-boat to target them if they zig-zag. But, of course, if we do get hit, it's all in order."

"I'm sure you're right, Baron Wolcinski," the answering voice was high and shrill and nervous-sounding. "My husband went into it most carefully. He would never have entrusted Elizabeth and me to a convoy unless he felt quite confident in our safety."

There was laughter above their heads.

"Mummy, I'm bored. Why can't I go and play with those children downstairs?"

"Because I promised Daddy that I would never let you out of my sight, Elizabeth, and they do look a little rough, dear. Now I'm just having a chat to Baron Wolcinski and then we'll go in and find your crayons."

"I'm bored with drawing on my own!"

Jimmy craned his neck back. He couldn't see anything, but then a gust blew and an edge of shiny pink ribbon blew over the railing above. He was sure it was the girl he'd seen eating in the dining room. He had been amazed at her skill with all those knives and forks.

Some of the kids with them had hardly used a knife and fork before, and even Sidney wiped his on the table-cloth to save the washing up. She'd looked so pretty and so knowing. Bored? Well, he wasn't bored. Not with Sidney and Keith around on deck.

"Of course, if the worst happened and we were hit, it would only be a ducking," went on the deep voice above. "And we might lose our luggage," said the man.

"Oh, of course," said the lady's voice, and she laughed with a tight, nervous sort of laugh. "But I never did much like swimming." And she laughed again.

"We've got the destroyer ahead watching out and two corvettes on the outside of the convoy, Mrs Wellington. The Germans can't get near us. But even if the unthinkable happened, we'd be picked up in minutes! It takes no time at all to launch the lifeboats from a modern ship like this."

"I suppose all these tiresome drills have their uses, Baron."

"Most certainly. And of course we've got all these poor children aboard. It's an excellent insurance for the non cabin-class passengers. The government is taking every care with this ship."

"Absolutely! I'm sure you're right. But I do find them a little off-putting in the dining room. I'm surprised they couldn't have found somewhere separate to feed them."

"I wish I could play with them. They are having such a good time."

"Oh, Elizabeth! Let's go and find something for you to do. We'll see you at luncheon, Baron, unless this sea gets any rougher. Then I am afraid I will just have to lie down."

"Now don't you worry any more, Mrs Wellington. The worst that can happen is an hour or two in a lifeboat . . ."

"An hour or two in a lifeboat," muttered Jimmy. The man was foreign and couldn't know what he was talking about. Surely they couldn't be torpedoed in a ship like the *Karachi*?

As the day wore on, the winds veered into violent, gusting squalls. Jimmy and Sidney and Keith ventured up again on deck but they could scarcely stand in the wind. The deck tilted first to one side and then to the other and they had to stand with their feet wide apart. No sooner was Jimmy balanced than a gust flung him against the rails and the waves rushed up to spray him. The ships in the convoy hurtled into view and then disappeared again in mountainous seas. If it was bad enough on a great liner like the *Karachi*, what must it be like in a ship a quarter of its size?

A Lascar sailor staggered down the deck towards them. He pointed at the boiling grey sea and angrily shooed them back in through the door leading below decks.

"I think he's saying it's dangerous," said Keith.

"He just don't want the bother of going overboard to get us," said Sidney lamely.

Jimmy forced out a laugh. Sidney was trying to be funny, but he wasn't funny.

They'd all three been strangely silent since they had overheard the conversation above their heads that morning. It had set a gloom over them. Perhaps the novelty of the ship had worn off. When you got used to it, you could only do so many things. If you couldn't get out on deck it was like being locked up in a very large house. Jimmy always played outside in the street with his gang. They never played inside – no mother in her right mind would have them indoors.

The constant heaving of the boat in the heavy seas was making him feel sick. They had none of them eaten much at lunch and some of the children's places had been empty.

Mr Barry wasn't proving much fun. He didn't seem to want to talk about his car racing. He and the other escorts had got more and more irritable since they left Liverpool, and not just bad-tempered with the children but snapping at each other too. At this rate they would be in a terrible state by the time they reached Canada.

"Let's go to the cabin," said Jimmy, after he and Sidney had started on their fourth game of snap. He was fed up with board games and he wasn't feeling at all good.

"Yeah," said Sidney, who was looking as yellow as he had that morning.

They walked over to a white-faced Keith, staring at the chessboard, and jerked their heads. Without a backward glance, Keith got up and followed them out. Silently they passed George and his mates in the passage. George stuck out a leg to a trip Jimmy up, but Jimmy just stepped over it. He felt a quick thrill of pleasure – George was feeling ill too.

They climbed on to the bunks and stared at the ceiling. Jimmy's stomach pitched and rolled in pace with the ship.

He was up like a flash, and made it – to the toilets. His stomach hurt and he was sick. He'd never been ill without Mum before. He brushed away the tears that had escaped from somewhere. Well, he'd better pull himself together and get used to it.

"You all right, Jimmy?" asked Sidney, his yellow face peering down from the top bunk.

"Yeah."

"I reckon someone's been at my money," said Keith slowly, lifting up his pillow. "I'm a penny ha'penny missing."

Sidney sat up and threw down his pillow: "Penny, twopence, threepence ha'penny, five, six, seven, eight, nine, ten, eleven, twelve. That's a shilling in coppers. And I've got two half crowns, and – blimey! – there's a threepenny bit missing, I know there is! Jimmy, what about yours, do you want me to count it?"

Jimmy shoved his hand under his pillow. He could feel a handful of smooth coins. He spread out his fingers, tracing all the creases in the sheet, but he could feel nothing sharp, nothing twisted, nothing like jagged metal.

"I don't know," he whispered, "but I think me German shrapnel's missing."

CHAPTER FIVE

"You keep it under your pillows?" Mr Barry asked absent-mindedly, staring out of the porthole. He seemed more interested in spying the destroyer ahead than hearing about the loss of their pocket money. "What can you expect? In this weather, with the pitching and the rolling, it's surprising there's any money left in place at all."

Jimmy had had a bad night. He had dreamt of Bob. He'd been falling and calling to Bob. Bob had looked round, straight at him, but he hadn't seen him. Jimmy kept falling and falling . . .

"And his lucky bit of shrapnel – that's gone too, mister," added Sidney.

"What's that Jimmy?" said Mr Barry. "Shrapnel!"

Jimmy could tell from Mr Barry's quick laugh that he wouldn't get any sympathy there.

"Nothin', mister," he muttered.

"If you can't look after your money, I'll take it in and keep a record for you. You can come and get it off me when you want it."

Jimmy thought about it. He'd never had pocket money in his life before. He'd only bought a ha'penny worth of boiled sweets since he'd been on board, but he liked looking at his money, counting it.

"I think that's a good idea, sir," said Keith. "We've got a problem here with our banking arrangements."

"Yeah," said Sidney. "Bank robbers, more like."

"Hand it over then," said Mr Barry.

He produced a notebook from his pocket. While the boys dug out and counted their money, he leant over Jimmy's bunk to peer out of the porthole.

"Don't that destroyer look small?" said Jimmy as he spotted it steaming so far away it looked a speck on the horizon. He held out nine shillings and seven pence.

"Smaller than the *Karachi*, yes, but it's done a splendid job!"

They all three felt better today, even Jimmy when he allowed himself to forget about his dream and the shrapnel. He was getting used to the rolling of the ship. He tried copying the sailors, walking with a wide-legged gait, and found it easier to keep his balance on the tilting deck. The wind still blew in violent gusts, and the sea and skies were still a leaden grey, but he liked the cold tang of the air and his appetite had returned for lunch.

Sidney had lost his sickly lemon colour. His eyes sparkled and his pale face was flushed pink with the wind. Every time they came to a barrier bar on deck, between the cabin class and the other class areas, Sidney tried a somersault over the railings. Light and springy, like a skinny length of bendy wire, he could shin or somersault over anything. Jimmy kept watch and told him when the coast was clear, while Keith marked the deck by scraping his black shoe hard.

"Another two inches," declared Keith. "If we can expand on that we'll soon have you in the Olympic team."

They had slipped out of the dining room at the end of lunch, before the first-class passengers had finished.

"Bet you can't get over into First Class," Jimmy said.

"Bet I can."

"Hold on," said Keith. "This might be a record, so it must be measured for posterity."

Keith paced out the steps.

"I reckon that's three feet six inches. Look – I'll mark it with my shoe."

"You've gotta take a deep breath, run up to the mark, let it out, jump and somersault the bar," said Jimmy, who was the trainer.

Sidney waited at the start line. Jimmy stood by as Keith knelt beside his black shoe mark.

"Ready!" Jimmy called, "steady . . . !"

From nowhere, a figure hurtled past, shoving Sidney back, and somersaulted over the bar.

"Hey!" Sidney shouted.

A Lascar sailor ran towards them shouting angrily at George, who was picking himself up off the deck. George flashed a smile of triumph at Jimmy and was gone. The sailor pounded up and waved the boys away, shaking his fist.

"Can you believe it!" said Jimmy. "Where did George come from?"

"Did you see how far he jumped," whistled Keith. "Three feet nine inches, I reckon!"

"Cheek, I call it," declared Sidney. "Show off!"

They gave up on Sidney's Olympic ambitions when they met a lady in navy slacks and a smart navy jacket, cut to look like a sailor's uniform. She was kneeling on the deck amid a tangle of cameras.

"Look at that!" said Keith. "How many have you got there?"

"Three." The lady was quite young and smiled with bright red painted lips.

"What are they for?"

"To film, of course."

"You're making a real film?" said Jimmy in awe. He was going to have so much to tell his parents when he wrote to them from Canada.

"Look here, if you boys aren't busy would you like to help me with the tripods? I could do with some assistants."

"What's this film about then?" asked Jimmy.

"It's not Mickey Mouse," the lady laughed. Her red lips looked out of place with her sailor's cap. "It's an official film. I expect it will go on the news at the cinema to make everyone jealous of you kids going off to Canada."

67

"Can I be in it?" said Jimmy doubtfully. He flattened down the wiry tufts on his head with one hand. Child star . . . Never in his wildest dreams had he . . .

"Of course. I think that will be too heavy for you," said the woman to Sidney as he tried to pick up the tallest tripod. "How about the boy over there?"

Jimmy turned. Lolling against the side of a cabin leant George. He sauntered forward and held out his arms for the tripod. Red in the face with effort, Sidney heaved the tripod up in his spindly arms.

"It's easy, miss. Leave it to me. I can do it – light as a feather."

"Are you sure?" said the lady doubtfully. "Well, would this boy be kind and carry my cameras. I need all the help I can get."

George picked up the cameras gingerly. Jimmy couldn't help feeling that George had got the best job. He must have been trailing them around. Strange he hadn't got some mischief going with his gang, but at least he couldn't get up to anything too awful with the lady around. To Jimmy's relief, George said not a word during the filming, and he even blushed when the lady thanked him.

At dinner that night all the children were back, over the worst of the sea sickness. The little ones no longer sat there white-faced, homesick and silent. They giggled and chattered and tucked into the food. The menus were gone. Instead the food was brought without comment and they all ate the same.

The Lascar stewards laughed and smiled with the children. Jimmy tried talking to the Lascar with a long black moustache who had smiled as he brought them all the food at their first meal.

"Me, Abdool. Leettle, leettle English. Me, children." He held up five fingers and pointed at himself.

"He means he's got five children," said Keith.

"I know that – I'm not stupid," said Jimmy. He might have been one of five if his brothers and sister had lived. He'd have liked that.

"What are you so quiet about, Jimmy?" called Mr Barry from across the table.

"Nothin', mister. Just thinkin'."

"No need for too much thinking now," Mr Barry said jovially. "We'll be in Canada this time next week – Montreal. It's a great country."

"Have you been there, sir?" asked Keith with interest.

"No, but it's a land on a scale you boys could hardly imagine. You're used to city streets, not space. Think of it – the towering Rockies, snow-bound north, areas of wheat as great as this sea around us, mighty rivers, empty lakes."

Jimmy sat listening. Space – that was what he had always wanted. Space to move and breathe. But he wouldn't half mind having Sidney and Keith with him.

"We'll stick together, we three, won't we?" he said.

"I'm going to me mum's cousin in Saskatchewan," said Sidney. "He works on a farm an' all, and 'e's got a 'orse and I'm goin' to ride it . . ."

"What about you then?" said Jimmy to Keith.

"I don't know," said Keith. "They only arranged for me to come at the last minute after . . . after . . ."

"Ain't you got any brothers and sisters?"

"My sister didn't . . . didn't . . ."

"My little sister died too, before the war. She wasn't half pretty. We'll stick together then. Perhaps we can get on the next-door farm to Sidney."

The escorts appeared to think this was funny, and roared with laughter. Jimmy stared furiously at Mr Barry, who caught his eye, stopped laughing and said, "How about you boys coming to the games room afterwards? I'll show you my photograph album of the races I've been in."

"Is it true, sir, that you built your own car?" said Keith.

"Took me two years."

"Crikey!" said Sidney.

It was the best evening yet. Mr Barry was surrounded by admiring children pushing and shoving to get a look at his photographs and to hear his stories. One of the escorts, a quiet young man in a clergyman's collar, held up each photograph in turn while Mr Barry explained about starting flags, rules of the track, near crashes. As the younger children gasped, the clergyman smiled a gentle, amused smile. Jimmy hadn't seen him before.

"How many preachers they got on this ship?" Jimmy nudged Keith. "I ain't seen that one before."

"Father O'Brien," said Keith. "He's a Catholic priest. He's been very sea sick until today."

"A priest," said Jimmy in a shocked voice. "My mum wouldn't like that. Fancy letting a priest come as an escort!"

"What's wrong with that?"

"We're chapel, strict chapel. My mum wouldn't be pleased if she knew we had Papists around. She says she'd rather have an honest Martian than a Papist any day."

"You'll have to do without me then."

"Blimey! Are you a Papist?"

"Yes."

"Come on, Jimmy, touch 'im – I dare you," said Sidney.

Papists were superstitious people who believed all sorts of mumbo-jumbo, Jimmy's mother had said. She must have got it wrong. You'd never get any mumbo-jumbo past Keith. Keith was the cleverest, clearest-thinking friend he'd ever had.

A smile spread slowly across Jimmy's face. When he was a little boy he was sure Mum knew everything in the world there was to know. She certainly had something to say on everything. He had never ceased to marvel at all she had to say. Now he wasn't so sure.

71

Perhaps when you grew up you thought things out differently.

"You won't catch me touchin' him. He's got horns and he might go up in smoke," said Jimmy grinning.

"Yes, I light the candles in church," said Keith.

"Candles? In church?" said Jimmy. Wonders would never cease. He'd never dare tell Mum.

That night Mr Barry came to supervise the cabins.

"You can get out of your clothes tonight, boys, and have a bath. Absolutely no fooling around in the bathroom, and put your pyjamas on afterwards, with your life jackets on top."

"But you said we had to sleep in our clothes, mister," said Jimmy, confused. "Why are we changin' now."

"Haven't you boys realised? This evening we sailed out of the danger zone. We're several hundred miles out into the Atlantic now – too far for enemy submarines to track us. We saw the naval escort leaving this afternoon, didn't we, Jimmy?"

Jimmy was puzzled. "The escort – you mean the destroyer?"

"And the corvettes too – they're busy warships. They're off to meet up with another convoy coming across from Canada, to accompany it back into Liverpool."

Jimmy remembered the tiny speck of the destroyer. He hadn't realised the naval escort would leave them.

"Most of the cargo ships in our convoy are empty. They'll sail on to Canada, load up with oil and wheat and food, and head straight back to England. It's not easy finding enough warships to police all these ships, so as soon as one convoy is out of danger, they have to make it fast to meet the next."

So that was why the children's escorts were all so jolly this evening! Since leaving Liverpool they'd been irritable and tense, pouncing on the children for the smallest things. Jimmy had felt conned by Mr Barry. He hadn't proved to be the friendly racing enthusiast he first appeared. Since they'd left port he had been so sharp with them. But tonight he had transformed back to the exciting Mr Barry, the daring racing-car driver.

Submarines . . . ! So they had been afraid of a U-boat attack all along. Jimmy had been afraid of air attacks, like back home, especially after he'd lost his shrapnel. How could he accuse Papists of being super-stitious? He'd been more superstitious than anyone. He hadn't given too much thought to submarines.

"Big ship like ours,"said Sidney proudly. "A torpedo 'ud 'ave gone in one side and out the other."

"But if it fired at a distance of . . ." began Keith.

"You could mend the 'oles easy, mister," went on Sidney. "Makin' racin' cars and all that – mendin' a 'ole would be a piece o' cake fer you."

"Well," laughed Mr Barry. "I'm glad not to have to try."

"He's not bad, is he?" whispered Jimmy as their cabin door was shut later.

"He's a nice man. I like him," agreed Keith.

"Look at that moon. I can see it from 'ere through the port'ole," said Sidney.

All three peered from their bunks. The moon was almost full, and from time to time it shone out over the heaving sea, until it was obscured by dark cloud again. The sea was still rough, crowned with white foam.

Jimmy watched for the moon's rays to break through a gap in the clouds, then he could see clearly the dark outlines of the ships sailing alongside them. It was beautiful. If he'd stayed in Union Street he'd never in a million years have seen something like this. He wriggled down in his bunk. It was warm and swayed up and down on the waves and he was sleepy . . .

The shuddering woke him. His bunk shook violently and he was thrown from its warmth. Heavy, muffled thuds deafened him, followed by the ear-splitting screech of metal, crashing glass and splintering wood.

Puzzled, Jimmy fell painfully onto the floor.

What was happening? He was cold. Instinctively, he tried to pull his blankets up, but they weren't there. He was clawing at hard floor, wet floor. His pyjamas were wet. Why was the floor wet?

"Blimey! – we've bin hit," came Sidney's voice.

Hit! No . . . Yes! Hit – by a torpedo? Jimmy couldn't think straight, he was still half asleep.

"Put a light on. Jimmy! Keith! We gotta get out."

The fog cleared in Jimmy's head. He crawled to the door and felt for the cabin light switch.

"It won't go on – it ain't workin'!"

Outside the crashing and cracking continued. Voices were shouting.

Sidney was already climbing down from the top bunk which was all askew. Jimmy leant back on his bunk. It was dark and his bedding was soaking wet. Was he awake?

The moon shone through the porthole and he could see that the water pipe running along the cabin beside his bed was fractured and spurting water.

Sidney was clambering down from his sloping bunk. If Keith didn't wake up soon he was going to get squashed underneath it. Keith was a hump hidden under his blankets.

"Wake up, Keith, we've been hit. We've got to get out."

Jimmy's eyes were adjusting to the faint light of the moon. He could make out the dark mound of shaking blankets. Keith was awake. Why didn't he get up?

"We've got to get 'im up, Sidney," yelled Jimmy.

Keith clutched at the blankets, but Jimmy and Sidney tore them away. Keith fumbled around for his glasses, shaking, and sat up.

"My glasses . . . I'm not going anywhere without my glasses."

Sidney and Jimmy desperately felt around the bunk.

A sharp pain pierced Jimmy in the foot. He gingerly put his hand down into the wet and felt the sharp edge of broken glass and the mangled wire frames.

"I'm not going without my glasses."

"I've got 'em in me pocket."

"You haven't got a pocket."

Outside voices were calling for help. The bell above the door began to ring, with a shrill, insistent pealing.

"We'll have to get help," said Jimmy desperately. "We'll not get 'im out alone."

"I will not go – I will not go . . ." said Keith like some mad automaton, shivering and hugging his knees as he spoke.

"Sidney – get the door open. We can drag 'im out between us."

Sidney felt his way to the cabin door and turned the handle. Then he put his foot against it and tugged. Finally he hammered at the door and tried again.

"Jimmy," he whispered, barely disguising the horror in his voice. "It's stuck. 'Ere – leave Keith. We gotta get this door open."

Together they tugged at the door. It wouldn't move, but the shrill bell above their heads went on ringing as if it would never stop. Jimmy ran his hand around the door frame.

"The door frame's skewed. It's all bent. The door won't open."

The floor of the cabin was beginning to tilt, not in

the backwards and forwards swaying motion of the waves, but in a permanent, sliding tilt.

"Holler, Sidney. We gotta shout . . ."

Together they hammered on the door and yelled and shouted. Their bell continued its shrill ring, while other bells replied in muffled, deadened tones. Distant shouts echoed down the corridor outside, doors were slammed and footsteps ran. It seemed ages before Jimmy felt the handle turn in his hand. Someone was on the other side, pushing.

"Pull, Sidney! There's someone there."

They shoved and pulled, water soaking their bare feet, faces grey in the light of the moon. Suddenly the door cracked open, swinging back to reveal an indistinct figure standing in the engulfing dark of the passage outside.

"Help us with Keith," cried Jimmy to their rescuer. "He's gone bonkers and we can't leave 'im."

They pulled and bullied Keith out of his bunk. He wouldn't speak to them and he wouldn't stand up. The water gushing from the pipe was inches deep now on the floor. Jimmy slipped as he tried to get hold of Keith round the waist, but Sidney grabbed him as he fell and helped shift Keith over their rescuer's back. With Jimmy lifting up Keith's legs behind, they climbed through the tilting door frame and into the blackness of the passage outside.

CHAPTER SIX

Despite the dark, there was no panic. They'd had enough drills so they knew what to do and where to go. Holding tightly on to Keith's legs, Jimmy joined the queue of calm but frightened children lining the passage and stairs. It was a bit like the queue at the pictures to see the Saturday-morning film.

The line moved slowly forward and the emergency lights came on. Soon afterwards a lady in a smart black suit and high-heeled sandals came clattering down the stairs. With her round, moon face, big blue eyes, and neatly waved grey-brown hair, Jimmy recognised her as one of the girls' escorts.

"It's only a torpedo, only a torpedo. Nothing to worry about," the woman called out. "Stay in line and follow the child in front of you."

Only a torpedo! So what else could be worse?

"Keith, I can't hold on much longer," said Jimmy. "I'm puttin' yer legs down. Yer'll have to walk."

Jimmy dropped Keith's legs.

"Is that boy hurt?" the woman in the black suit asked, her anxious blue eyes darting from child to child.

"No he's not," Jimmy said. "He's not bothered to stand."

"Go ahead, keep moving. I've got to find my girls," she called as she disappeared out of sight along the passage.

"Go on – stand!" ordered Sidney. "Yer can't expect Jimmy and this man to carry you."

Keith tried to put his weight on his feet, but his legs buckled beneath him. He clung on to his rescuer's back.

"They won't stand," he whispered. "Leave me – I don't want to come."

"Yer don't want to come!" yelled Sidney. "One more word out of you and I'm going to 'it you – 'ard – in the gob."

"Come on, Keith," said Jimmy wearily picking up Keith's feet as the children moved up the stairs. "Sidney, you take one leg, and I'll take the other."

On deck the wind was blowing fiercely and the ship was heaving worse than usual. She was balanced at a strange angle, listing to one side, and sloping down towards the bows.

The bright moon slid in and out from behind the stormy black clouds, illuminating pale, barefoot figures in pyjamas and life jackets walking quickly in their lines. Sailors hurried them along to their lifeboat stations, carrying some of the sleepy smaller children in their arms.

Now Jimmy could see that part of the ship had been blown away, near the stern and beside their cabins. A gaping hole had opened in the side, blowing the deck above their cabins away. They skirted the shattered deck. Flickering little flames were licking at its jagged edges and a strange smell, like the smell of a newly lit match, hung in the air. Without warning a fountain of thundering water and spray shot up through the hole and out on to the deck. There was water in the ship all right. The sooner they got into the boats and were picked up by the rest of the convoy the better!

Sidney mouthed at Jimmy, but his voice was lost on the screaming wind.

"It's all right, Sidney," Jimmy yelled in Sidney's ear. "It's not much water . . . We'll make it round."

"No . . . Babs. Where's Babs?" Sidney yelled back.

"With her escort of course," said Jimmy. He tried to sound as confident as he could. "Hold on to Keith."

The deck was definitely tilting, and not just with the waves, and it was listing more sharply than when they had first got on deck. Jimmy stared out over the sea. They'd be all right on a tanker. He'd always wanted to see inside a tanker.

The waves were too high to see the other ships – but they should be able to see them. Jimmy craned and screwed up his eyes. Now and again he saw the outline of a dark shape, but they were getting smaller, moving away.

"Sidney?" Jimmy yelled. "You see the convoy?"

Sidney stared. "They're . . . No, Jimmy! They're . . ."

"Come on!" yelled Jimmy. "Let's get a move on."

Together with their rescuer, they lugged and hauled Keith round the deck towards their station. One lifeboat had already been launched on the black, heaving sea. Men slid down a rope into the boat and coaxed little children after them. Metal winches scraped and wooden sides creaked as other boats were lowered.

"Quick!" shouted Jimmy. Surely they wouldn't leave without them. "They're goin' already."

Before their eyes another boat was launched into the teeming waves, but it seemed to have been mistimed. The waves sunk away faster than the boat could be lowered. It hovered for a minute, its winch chains uneven, and then capsized. There were screams of children, followed by a shower of rafts and life belts thrown down from the deck.

Jimmy, Sidney and Keith's rescuer broke into a run. Their boat was still at its station.

"Last one to go," called a voice. "Climb in boys."

The boys were thrown roughly in among a mass of bodies. Where was Mr Barry? Jimmy hadn't seen him since they'd gone to bed.

"All ready now – hold on! What's that lady doing? Last boat, madam."

"But you can't leave . . . I can't get to my girls. They aren't in their cabins.

Jimmy peered up from the mound of bodies and saw the lady in the black suit trying to pull her arm away from an officer.

"They'll have been taken care of. Don't you worry."

"But I can't leave without knowing – I'm responsible for them."

"Listen, lady, this ship's going down, sinking!"

"But I can't . . . ."

The officer gazed sternly into the boat.

"Madam, these boys we've just put in – we've got others in here too – they're all alone. Who's going to supervise them, I ask you?"

The woman stared round wildly until she caught Jimmy's eye. "Are you alone?"

"Yes," Jimmy shouted. He didn't know if they were alone. He hadn't seen Mr Barry, but he wanted the lady in the boat. At this rate, they'd never get off. To his relief she climbed in.

"Clear away the boat," yelled the officer. "Man the falls and stand by for lowering."

The boat descended jerkily to the waves. The waves must have fallen back as, for a moment, the boat was left dangling in the air. The front dropped and they hung at a horrendous angle, staring at the black, foaming waves beneath them.

"Hold on!" the lady called to them. As if they wouldn't!

Jimmy clung to the edge of a bench as tightly as a monkey. The boat righted and they hit water. The waves tore and slapped at the boat but they were still attached to the liner by a rope.

Jimmy looked up at the liner towering over them,

sloping at a drunken angle. Above his head the heavy iron launching gear swung backwards and forwards, threatening to brain anyone who stood up.

Jimmy could never have stood up, jammed in as he was. Above them people were still throwing life rafts off the *Karachi* and jumping overboard after them. Despite the screaming of the wind and the screams of people still on the ship and in the sea, Jimmy felt as if he might be at the pictures after all. He was numb. Squeezed in as tight as he was, he couldn't feel his body, his feet or hands. He couldn't even feel his mind. He was numb through and through.

They were cast off from the ship and they drew away from the liner's bright lights. The waves had looked big from the deck of the ship, but now, as the lifeboat sank down on the sea, they looked like mountains. One moment the lifeboat sank into a dark valley, cut off from the world, with towering black walls of sea above them, and the next moment she was tossed up on foaming crests with the liner in view.

The moon slid in and out of the stormy clouds. When it shone out Jimmy could see other lifeboats tossing on the waves. One was hurled past upside down, here and there a raft laden with bodies shot past, or a light flashed from a passing torch. Sometimes a shout rose above the wind's screaming. Sometimes a figure slipped by the boat and was hauled aboard, dripping ice-cold water.

Jimmy suddenly glimpsed a small pale head.

"There's a baby," he yelled, pointing and tugging at the people around him.

The waves tossed up the small shape with its pale face, alongside the boat.

"No – it's a girl's china doll," shouted a man close by.

Jimmy turned but he couldn't see Sidney in the mass of bodies. He hoped he hadn't heard.

Jimmy could feel the sway of bodies as men frantic-ally heaved backwards and forwards in the middle of the boat.

"Put your backs into it . . . We're doing well . . . Keep going. Got to get her away before the ship sinks. We're not going down with her!" yelled a voice encouragingly.

From time to time figures moved and different men took the place of the men heaving in the middle. Each time the boat rose on the crest of a wave, the liner, ablaze with her emergency lights, was a little further away and a little lower.

Jimmy wasn't sure how long he clung there before a horrified cry went up: "Oh no!"

Jimmy craned his neck and peered where everyone was looking. They were quite far out now. The great liner had upended and was sinking slowly into the black sea, every light blazing. And then she was gone, as if she had never been, swallowed up by the raging waves.

There were voices around Jimmy: voices that floated in and out of the whine of the wind, and the hammering of the sea.

"We'll be picked up soon."

"The convoy's scattered. Didn't you see them go?"

"Gone?"

"Yes, madam. Convoy rules. If there's an attack, all ships scatter and make it alone."

"But . . ."

"If they stayed to pick us up, they'd be obvious targets for the attacking U-boat."

"But that's inhumane!"

"Losing more ships, more lives – is that humane?"

"The destroyer – won't that come back? We have the children!"

"Don't worry, madam. The *Karachi* will have radioed before she sunk, but in these conditions I doubt they'll get the destroyer to us before the morning."

"There's a lot of sea they've got to search," broke in a deep foreign voice, "if they are to collect all the survivors."

Other voices were interwoven, voices talking urgently to each other in a strange language.

"It's cold! September in an Atlantic storm – not my idea of a holiday," the lady's voice dropped to a whisper. "These children, they've only got pyjamas under their life jackets."

Jimmy realised for the first time that the adult bodies around him were fully dressed. The ship must have been hit soon after the children fell asleep, before the grown-ups had gone to their cabins. That's why Mr Barry hadn't been there. He must still have been in the lounge.

"Come on now – pull! Pull! We've got to keep her head on to the waves. We can't have her swamping. Watch out!"

Another lifeboat appeared from nowhere alongside, crammed with a mass of bodies.

A man stood up and cupped his hands and shouted across to the other boat: "Seen the destroyer about?"

"In the morning," came the faint answering voice. "Good luck!"

A man waved and the other boat moved away.

No one spoke again, except for an officer at the front shouting out orders to the men heaving in the centre. Jimmy couldn't see oars. The men seemed to be pulling at two rows of handles like upright truncheons. There must have been five lots of handles, set between the seats. The men heaved backwards and forwards and the boat moved on, struggling to keep head on to the waves. Even Jimmy could see that if they drifted side on, a wave could submerge them in a moment.

All through the night the men moved around, taking turns at the handles. From time to time a slight, thin man dived off the boat. There were shouts of encouragement as he was pulled back aboard, dragging another body with him. Again and again the same man went back for more and the boat became yet tighter and more squashed.

Jimmy couldn't think; he didn't sleep. He stared at the leg in his lap, Keith's leg he supposed. He was squeezed in so tight that hard edges dug into him, and cold bodies threatened to smother him. Something sharp was digging into his thigh, but he didn't feel it. It hurt, but it was as if it hurt someone else, someone who had nothing to do with the numb body he occupied.

"They'll be here soon."

"Of course they will . . . They'll have got word of it by now. The other ships in the convoy will have radioed back too."

"The search planes will be out at dawn."

Gradually the dark lightened into shades of chill grey. Jimmy could see clearly now the white foam on the lashing waves. The boat seemed like a toy, tossed on the mountainous wave crests until it sank again into sullen hollows, showered with freezing spray. As they rose up again, Jimmy glimpsed wave after wave racing towards them on the grey sea, stretching away into a grey horizon.

There wasn't a single boat or ship in sight, not even a raft. Now and again a bit of wreckage floated past but otherwise the sea and sky were empty. They were alone, the convoy a dream of yesterday, with only the rising seas and the screaming wind.

"Blimey!" came a whisper from a head which popped up beside him.

"Sidney!"

And Keith – where was he?

Jimmy's eyes worked in a line from the blue foot resting on his lap, up a pyjama-striped leg, to a pale face with grey, blank eyes, naked without their glasses.

"Keith . . . you all right?"

Keith didn't look at Jimmy and didn't answer.

"Is he all right then?" Jimmy said, tapping the back against which Keith was propped.

Keith flopped sideways as the back twisted round, and Jimmy found himself staring into the fierce dark eyes of George.

CHAPTER SEVEN

"Attention everyone! Can you hear me down there?" The deep voice, borne by the wind, floated down to Jimmy from the back of the boat. "Put your arms in the air if you can hear me."

A youngish man, tall, with a beaky nose, and hair cut very short at the sides, was standing at the stern. He wore a sodden naval uniform.

"As the most senior officer here, I am now in charge of this boat."

The faces around Jimmy were attentive, with obvious relief.

"I am Lieutenant Ingram and I shall be manning the tiller together with my junior colleague, Petty Officer Hamilton."

The thin, boyish form of Petty Officer Hamilton bobbed up briefly. Jimmy recognised him as the man who had dived overboard so many times in the night, pulling aboard people from the sea. He didn't look much older than the oldest boys at school.

"We also have aboard the senior steward of the *Karachi* who will be in charge of provisions. We have adequate water and emergency rations, more than enough, as we should be picked up by nightfall tonight.

To help Petty Officer Hamilton and myself we also have Gunner Mackenzie aboard."

Excited chatter broke out among the boys.

"What's a tiller?" said Sidney.

"I dunno," said Jimmy.

"That bit of wood, I expect," muttered George over his shoulder.

Jimmy jumped – he'd never heard George speak in any but a taunting voice before.

"It's a means of steering," murmured Keith.

Sidney and Jimmy stared at him. So he *was* all there after all, and he was listening. Jimmy looked at Sidney and put his fingers to his lips to silence him.

"Well I dunno," he said. "Don't look like a steering wheel to me. It's a pump, like the ones at home in the street. You pump it up and down and the fresh water comes out."

"No, Jimmy," said Sidney with one eye on Keith. "It's not for water. It's a pump-action machine gun. It fires out the back, don't it, Keith?"

Keith pulled himself upright. "I haven't got my glasses. I can't see that far, but if it's a tiller it's got to be for steering. It will be attached to the rudder at the back, and if you turn it to the left the rudder will move to the opposite side, controlling the direction of the . . ."

Jimmy was smiling at Sidney. He was relieved. You'd have thought Keith was dead if he hadn't been breathing. He caught George watching him and Sidney with a curious expression in his eyes, eyes which then turned back to Keith.

Lieutenant Ingram was shouting again.

". . . naval men and steward to the stern, Lascars in the mid section and I want all children and other passengers from the *Karachi* up in the bows."

The woman in the smart black suit got up carefully and climbed awkwardly over the bodies down to the front of the boat. Her wavy hair had lost its sleekness and gone all frizzy and her suit was creased and stained with damp spots. She called to the boys to follow her and they clambered over legs and were handed down by helping arms.

Jimmy, Sidney, Keith and George sat down close up against each other. Jimmy wouldn't have believed there could be room for anyone else, but two younger boys, hands tightly clasped, were handed down after them. Jimmy remembered having seen them in the dining room with the younger group. They were dark, curly-haired twins. They couldn't be more than eight.

"Phew!" They were so squashed Jimmy felt he'd never be able to take a proper breath.

There was shouting of instructions as a thick-set, heavy man with bristly brown hair cut very short shoved and pushed his way down the boat. In his arms he held a wet green bundle.

"Lean back. Careful! Her wee arm's broken!"

"Pass her to the lady escort."

Both the lady escort and Jimmy looked up in

surprise. At one end of the bundle were some pink-flowered pyjama legs while the other end trailed rats' tails of wet brown hair, scraped together by a be-draggled pink ribbon that hung limply over a green velvet collar.

"Compliments of Petty Officer Hamilton," said the thick-set sailor in naval uniform. "Pulled the lassie from the sea last night, he did. And ye watch what you're doing with her – her arm's broken."

The lady escort looked rather taken aback at being ordered around by the sailor.

"Of course I shall take care of her, Gunner Mackenzie, and as best we can in these circumstances," she said in a clear, calm voice.

Jimmy stared at the white face with its blue-white lips that lay on the lady's lap. It was that girl all right. It didn't matter if you were rich and travelling first class, or poor and going cabin class; when it came to torpedoes you were all equal.

Jimmy looked beyond her and counted at least twenty Lascars, some in the tight, buttoned stewards' jackets with blue sashes stained dark by the sea, and some in cooks' outfits. The boat must have been stationed near the kitchens. They drew themselves together in the centre of the boat, chattering among themselves in their own language.

Laid at the feet of the Lascars was a prone body.

"Who's that?" whispered Sidney.

"I dunno," said Jimmy.

"I think it's Father O'Brien," said Keith, blinking. "He's sick."

When they were all settled, and Jimmy was convinced there wasn't an inch of space left anywhere, a big man in a black bow tie, heavy overcoat and black Homburg hat, forced himself in along beside the boys. They stared at him.

"He's not cabin class," muttered Sidney in Jimmy's ear.

The man caught sight of the lady escort, took off his hat and made a little bow in her direction with his head.

"Frederik Wolcinski," he said.

"Isabel Cavendish," the lady escort nodded back.

As everyone settled, chattering broke out on all sides. It was such a relief to see daylight and to be alive and well. Jimmy grinned as Sidney leant towards him.

"What 'ud yer rather be," said Sidney triumphantly, "bombed at 'ome or torpedered in the Atlantic?"

"Torpedered!" said Jimmy. "Think what we'll tell the kids at school."

Keith collapsed down on his seat, leaning against George.

"Yer heavy," shouted George. "Sit up!"

Jimmy realised their mistake. Keith had been both bombed and torpedoed, all in the space of a week.

"Go on, get off," yelled George. "You've 'alf broke me back last night as it is . . . Now, get off!"

As Keith pulled himself upright with the same blank

expression on his face, Jimmy watched, open-mouthed.

"It were you then. You carried Keith!"

"Bloody great weight – ruined me back," said George. "At least it weren't you, with yer fat . . ."

"Did you push our door open and carry Keith?" persisted Jimmy. "Did you –"

"Ah – shut up! 'Alf ruined me back. It hurts somethin' 'orrible."

The elation in the boat was infectious. Baron Wolcinski told Miss Cavendish interminable stories of every liner he had ever been on, but Miss Cavendish looked too happy to be bored. Then Miss Cavendish got a game of I-spy going. Although they had a spot of bother finding colours other than grey and black, they managed pink (hair ribbon) and green (coat), which raised a smile out of Elizabeth. The Lascar stewards chatted non-stop among themselves.

The Lascars took it in turns with the naval men to work the handles in the centre of the boat. They weren't oars, Keith had explained, but hand levers, and it looked as if they were driving a shaft, running along the bottom of the boat, to a propeller at the stern. Jimmy and Sidney sat happily through Keith's long explanation about how each pair of handles, working backwards and forwards, was obviously turning the shaft leading to the propeller, and sending the boat forward. It wasn't obvious to Jimmy at all, but it was good to hear Keith talking again.

George had his back turned and seemed not to be listening until, "Well – I can't see how the propeller moves us forward?" he asked Keith.

The steward came down the boat and shared out blankets. There weren't enough to go round so they had to share.

"Cold, are you, boys?" He was a round, friendly man with a soft voice. "Just pyjamas and life jackets? You hug up to each other under these, and you'll be as warm as toast. Won't be long now till they pick us up and we can all have a hot bath."

Jimmy, in his numbness, hadn't thought about the cold. Now he thought about it, he knew he was very cold. His bare feet were like blocks of ice. It was good they were squeezed in so tight. It kept the wind and draughts off.

The steward clambered back with a flapping armful of canvas.

"Give me a hand, son," he said to Jimmy. "Hold it down for me."

Jimmy stood up to take the other end and they held it down while the steward unwound a reel of rope and tied the canvas down to make a shelter over the bows.

"That's grand, it is!" said Sidney.

"Yeah," said Jimmy fixing his corner. "Good as a tent. Wouldn't mind having a night under that."

"No, lads. We're putting the girl and those little ones out of the wind."

"I bet we'll be in boring bunk beds again tonight."

"They won't be boring – we'll be on a destroyer," said Sidney.

Despite the high winds and waves the boat was like a holiday outing – everyone laughing and smiling and chatting. They'd survived the night after all.

"Shame we won't get to sleep under that," said Jimmy as he surveyed the canvas shelter.

" 'Ope we get picked up before supper," said Sidney. "I'm starvin'."

Jimmy didn't like to say he was starving too. He didn't want any more 'fatty' taunts. He glanced across at George and their eyes met.

"You starvin' too?" he said cautiously.

"Yeah," said George, glancing out to sea. "I could eat an 'orse."

Jimmy laughed. "And I could eat an elephant – I really could."

It was midday before the steward brought the first food: one sardine each on a hard, dry biscuit, and a drink of water from a metal dipper. The dipper was much narrower than a glass and Jimmy drank all the water it held and he was still thirsty.

"That did all right then?" said Sidney, smacking his lips.

George was still munching his way through his

biscuit, carefully examining his navy life jacket to pick off every crumb. He certainly knew how not to waste a bit, thought Jimmy. Mum would approve of that. Come to think of it, he wouldn't mind seeing Mum before he set off to Canada again.

"A quarter of a pint," said Keith.

"What are you on about?" said Jimmy. "I ain't seen no pints round here."

"Of water," Keith explained. "I estimate that that is a quarter-pint dipper for the water. He's rationing it. We're getting a quarter of a pint each."

The boys chattered cheerfully among themselves. George appeared to have got out first. He had never gone to sleep but had been up to something in his cabin when he heard and felt the full impact of the torpedo. As far as Jimmy could make out from George's brief account, George had gone along the corridor, opening the doors into the cabins to wake everyone, that was how he'd heard them banging. It made Jimmy shiver to think what would have happened if George hadn't heard them.

The two younger boys with the black curls smiled and said "Dunno" to every question.

"They're a bit stupid, ain't they," said Sidney. "Lost their memory or somethin'. Come on – what's yer names then."

The boys looked at each other. "Dunno."

"I think they're called Daniel and Jacob," said Miss Cavendish.

"Daniel and Jacob, is it?" said Sidney.

The two boys began to cry.

"Leave 'em," said Jimmy. "I reckon it's their nerves." He knew about nerves as his mum sometimes had them. If you left her for a bit they usually went away.

Elizabeth, the girl in the green coat, one arm tied to her body with a piece of rope, sat leaning against Miss Cavendish. She was listening to their stories all right, but Jimmy didn't dare talk to her. Where was her mum, the one who didn't like swimming?

They soon exhausted all their stories of getting off the *Karachi*. Miss Cavendish, who turned out to be a music teacher, organised a singsong. They got through *Run, Rabbit, Run* with all the boat joining in except the Lascars, who at first looked as if they thought everyone had gone barmy, but who then listened with smiles on their faces. They went on to *Roll out the Barrel*, and then *There'll Always be an England*; it was one of Mum's favourites and Jimmy's throat tightened too much to sing.

The singing trailed off and Miss Cavendish tried in vain to encourage them to sing on.

"It's making me thirsty," explained George.

"I've had enough singin'," said Sidney.

Gunner Mackenzie barged down the boat to check the awning as the boys settled back to rest after the effort of the singsong.

"Haveni' ye got these bairns organised?" shouted the gunner to Miss Cavendish. "I dunno." And he shook his head. "Where they found these escorts beats me."

Miss Cavendish frowned and opened her mouth to speak, "We've just had a singsong. You must have . . ."

The gunner ignored her and went on shaking his head.

"Ye must keep the weans alert and active. Now one of ye laddies get beside the mast and hang on aye and give a shout when ye see land, a Sunderland airplane for that mind."

The gunner pulled Jimmy up roughly and shoved him so that he fell against several Lascars as he got to the mast. He clasped the rough wood with one arm and looked out. Gulls soared by with beaks open. He couldn't hear their screeches though, drowned as they were by the wind, and by the creaking of the mast.

It was good to stretch his legs after being cramped up all night, but just as his legs became exhausted with the effort of keeping upright in the rolling boat, George appeared to take his place.

"Seen anythin'?" shouted George.

What a question? If he'd seen anything he'd have yelled his head off.

"Wish I 'ad!"

"I'll keep watch now," said George importantly. "You can go back."

From the way George said it you would have thought the whole boat depended on his watch.

George's face was alive and alert in a way Jimmy had never noticed before.

The light began to fade. Somehow the day had slipped by. Jimmy felt the air getting colder, and wind rising, ruffling up his thick hair. Where was the destroyer? Surely it should have been there by now? In the boat they had lapsed into silence. The relief at being alive and surviving the sinking had evaporated long ago and no one chattered any more.

Jimmy felt a nudge.

"Do you think we'll be picked up tonight?" said Sidney.

Jimmy looked expectantly at Miss Cavendish. He was sure she had heard the question, but she gazed over their heads into the distance.

"I mean – I've been lookin' an' lookin' at the horizon and I ain't seen a bit of smoke from a ship, and I've watched the sky . . . A Sunderland like, it's a big plane, ain't it, Keith? And I knows I'd 'ave seen it so . . ."

"How big is a Sunderland then, Keith?" asked Jimmy. He'd been thinking the same thoughts as Sidney, but it disturbed him to hear them said out loud. If they were spoken they seemed more real than if they were just thoughts.

"Big," said Keith unhelpfully. "We've drifted too far away – it's obvious. The planes and search ships will

100

have been there, but they've missed us. The sea's an enormous place, a vast area. It's very difficult to find and spot an isolated boat, especially when we're hidden by these waves."

Keith spoke with an edge of triumph in his voice. Why did he say all that, thought Jimmy? It might be true but he didn't have to say it. The trouble with Keith was that he'd been hit too hard already. He was stuffed full of gloomy facts. He expected the worst. He didn't want to hope.

Jimmy stared at Sidney's wobbling face. He couldn't believe it. Sidney was crying. Streams of silent tears were flowing down his face.

"What's up, Sid?" said Jimmy desperately, offering his sleeve to dry the tears on Sidney's face. "Keith's a clever clogs but he can't always be right now, can 'e?"

George was staring at Sidney with a mixture of horror and amazement on his face.

"Course 'e's not right," George burst in. "We'll get back, I know we will. Even if we're not picked up tonight we'll do it – we'll make it out. There's gotta be a way somehow."

Sidney's tears streamed on Jimmy's proffered sleeve.

"It's Babs," he whispered. "She's only little and I promised Mum I'd look after her."

Jimmy hesitated, unsure what to say.

"Look at *her*!" shouted Sidney suddenly, pointing at Elizabeth who was watching him from the other side. "She don't belong 'ere. She weren't in our group. It's a boys' group. It should 'ave been Babs if we'd 'ad a girl – she's taken Babs' place."

"Come on, Sidney," said Jimmy. "You know that ain't fair."

"I know those sort," went on Sidney. "Me dad's a communist and 'e warned me about them lot. Think they can buy their way in anywhere."

"Sidney, that ain't true and you know it. That officer fished her out of the sea last night. Did you want 'im to leave her?"

Sidney lowered his head and cried again.

"Sorry," he whispered. "Sorry."

"Give him this," said George.

He held out a clenched fist. Something sharp and cold was pushed into Jimmy's hand. Jimmy opened his fist and stared. Then he closed it again and pushed his hand into Sidney's.

"There you are! You have this now."

Sidney examined the blackened piece of metal that lay in his hand.

"Jimmy's shrapnel," he whispered in disbelief. He sniffed and sat up, "Blimey! This is lucky, this is!"

CHAPTER EIGHT

That night there weren't enough blankets to go round. Miss Cavendish said she didn't need one as she was too busy settling the children in her care to feel the cold.

She settled Sidney, Keith, Jimmy and George on top of the cupboard at the front of the boat. She called it the locker in the bows. Its top was flat like a deck surface. They tried to curl round each other and keep the two blankets on. Sometimes Jimmy or George – they were the biggest – would dislodge the blanket with a jerking leg, then they all woke up and tried to rearrange themselves. Elizabeth, Daniel and Jacob were squeezed below, inside the locker, out of the wind.

Jimmy didn't sleep much and he didn't think the other boys did either. The spray showered over the boat, stinging his face, and however well he tucked in the blanket he was always cold. His feet were freezing enough, but whenever Sidney's bony legs and toes landed on him they felt like icicles.

For another thing, he couldn't sleep because of the endless rolling of the boat. One moment he was thrown to one side and another moment to the other.

Sidney called out for his mum and woke them all.

Another time Keith sat bolt upright, pulling the blankets off with him, and gabbled something about wishing he were dead, until George told him that if he didn't have any better plans he should shut his gob.

Once they were all woken by the gunner. He stumbled across their legs out of nowhere.

"Here, what's all this?" he growled. "This bairn's got no blanket on. No wonder he's cold, poor wee wretch. Come on, laddie, let's tuck the blanket under – that's the way – ought to be someone keepin' an eye on these bairns."

The gunner glared fiercely at Miss Cavendish and departed as abruptly as he had come. But Miss Cavendish never seemed to sleep. Whenever Jimmy woke she was there, helping rearrange their legs or tuck in their blankets.

"It's all right. Try to sleep now." Her calm voice was like a comforting refrain, soothing away their nightmares. But she couldn't drown out the noise of the slapping waves, the shriek of the wind, and the mast's groaning. To Jimmy, the night went on for ever.

Morning came and the boys sat up to stretch their cold and aching legs.

"George, you're a big chap," said Miss Cavendish. "Would you mind holding a blanket for Elizabeth and myself."

" 'Old a blanket?" said George, rubbing his arms. "The chief steward has just told us to fold 'em up."

"Just do as you are asked, please, George. Jimmy, will you take the other end?"

The penny suddenly dropped with Jimmy.

"It's the bucket, George," he hissed.

George blushed bright red, as did Elizabeth. The flush lit up her pale face, making her look almost healthy. It was all right for them, Jimmy realised – they could piss in the bucket – but it wasn't half complicated being a girl.

The blanket finished with and put away, Miss Cavendish tied her handkerchief to a piece of string from the locker and dangled it over the edge into the sea. Then she passed the wet handkerchief round the boys to wipe their faces and hands. It took a long time to pass it round all of them, rinsing in the sea between each boy.

Baron Wolcinski looked on with disgust as George tried to pass him the handkerchief. Instead he pulled a newspaper from inside his coat, dampened it and wiped it round his face and hands.

"They're sure to come today," said Sidney, his tears of the previous day forgotten.

"Course they are," said Jimmy.

Keith stared gloomily ahead.

The ferocity of the wind had diminished to a steady breeze.

"What's 'e up to then?" said Sidney, nodding towards Petty Officer Hamilton. The young petty officer was expertly hauling some canvas up the mast.

"It's a sail!" shouted George. "See what I mean – yer got to think of somethin', work it out and then we'll get there."

"Where?" said Keith.

Jimmy stared at Keith. What was he on about now?

"I mean *where* is *there*?" added Keith gloomily.

"I dunno," said Jimmy. "Eh, mister," he called to the young officer, "where we makin' for?"

Petty Officer Hamilton didn't speak until he had the sail hoisted and tied. Then he turned and grinned, the wind blowing the long brown strands of hair that flopped round his forehead.

"We're going east, to Ireland."

"Do they teach you 'ow to sail in the navy?" asked Sidney.

"No," the petty officer smiled. "But I've had a dinghy all my life. At your age I knew all about sailing."

"On yer own?" said Sidney.

"With a crew, or sometimes on my own."

"Good thing we've got you in the boat then," said Jimmy, suddenly feeling a lot happier.

George listened, an expression of wistful envy on his face. "I wouldn't mind a boat of me own," he said.

"I've got one." It was Elizabeth's high voice. "Actually, it's my grandfather's, and it's bigger than a dinghy, more of a yacht really."

"You would 'ave," muttered Sidney fiercely. Elizabeth glared at him.

They'd taken against each other all right, thought Jimmy, but at least that showed they were feeling better.

"It's no use sailing, if you can't navigate," said Keith.

"We've got a compass and the stars, and with a bit of luck the sun – what more do you want?" laughed the petty officer.

"But have you got a bearing on where we started from, or the point at which we are now?" said Keith.

The petty officer had stopped listening. He adjusted the sail.

The boat drove forward at a fine speed. Jimmy looked back at the little huddle of naval men around the tiller. Their faces were expressionless, revealing nothing, but with the speed they were now moving it certainly felt as if they were getting somewhere.

"Perhaps we'll make it to Ireland before they find us," he said.

"Course we will," said George.

Jimmy hadn't been talking to anyone in particular. He was surprised when George agreed with him, but then he was surprised how much talking George had been doing. Before he thought to check himself, Jimmy turned to George with a smile. He could have kicked himself!

Jimmy loved the rush of the boat as the wind filled the sail. He tried to ignore the gnawing hunger and thirst he felt eating away at his stomach.

"We should have kept some of that Victory Sponge for emergency rations," Jimmy said wistfully.

He remembered that first night when they had stuffed themselves full, working their way through the complete menu. He could hardly bear to think of it now.

"Made an ass of yerself," said George nastily. "Greedy guts . . ."

"Now look 'ere," announced Sidney, drawing his thin back up to full height. "I know you got us out and helped Keith, but Jimmy 'ere is my friend and it's no good goin' on like that now we're all stuck in this boat . . ."

Jimmy was grateful for Sidney's help, but he looked a lot like the boy David challenging the giant Goliath.

"He's right, George," Jimmy ventured. "Me, Sidney and Keith here – we're all mates." George's face tightened and his eyes blazed angrily. "If you want to be our mate too," Jimmy struggled on, "I'd like that, I really would. Wouldn't you Sidney, Keith?"

Keith grunted and Sidney stared at George doubtfully and then nodded slowly. They all watched George. Then Jimmy held out his hand and George grasped it.

"That's all right then, ain't it?" said Jimmy.

The blaze had gone from George's eyes and he didn't seem to know where to look.

"Know what I'm going to 'ave when I land," said

George suddenly. "Sausages for breakfast and roast beef and Yorkshire pudding for dinner."

"We only have roast beef for Christmas dinner," said Jimmy, "but it don't 'alf taste good."

"I've had roast beef once," said George proudly, "when me dad was in work."

"What's he do – your dad?" asked Jimmy.

George gazed intently at the waves.

"'E's – 'e's left," he said so savagely that Jimmy jumped.

Miss Cavendish got another I-spy game going with them. It was good fun at first, but they soon started running out of things to spy. There was the boat and all that there was in it, but apart from that there was only sea and sky and clouds. Only Keith got more and more involved, thinking of the most unusual things, like metal rivets in the mast that nobody could see anyway. The game petered out and they sat in silence.

"I can't wait to see Mum and Dad's faces when I walk in," said Jimmy.

He had been thinking of home. What would his mother be doing now? His father would either still be asleep after a night shift or out on the trains, but his mum would be in the kitchen scrubbing the floor before her shift at Mr Rothstein's place, or perhaps she was walking down Union Street to the factory. Perhaps she was thinking about Jimmy.

"I wish I could take Mum back a present," said Jimmy. Being away from her he realised now how much he depended on Mum and missed her. "But I left me pocket money with Mr Barry. I hope he's keepin' it safe."

"I never 'ad no pocket money before," said Sidney. "I could've got me mum some of those boiled sweets, like you got, Jim. She'd've liked those. Yer mum like boiled sweets, George?"

Jimmy was pleased. Sidney was trying to be friendly to George and it wasn't easy when he'd been such a bully before.

The blaze returned to George's eyes.

"I dunno. But she's not 'aving any from me, and that's for sure."

George was strange, thought Jimmy. He'd never met someone so quick to anger and over such ordinary things.

"When you's home, you –"

"I'm not goin' 'ome!"

"Where you goin' then?" said Sidney with interest.

At all this talk of mothers Keith had sat stock still, expressionless like a statue. What an ass he was! thought Jimmy. Why had he brought up the subject of mothers? Not only Keith, but George too now. Mothers were a dangerous subject.

"Look," said Jimmy quickly, "what's the gunner up to, then?"

The gunner had peeled off all his clothes and was

110

standing on the edge of the boat. His big square body looked like that of a pink, lumbering whale.

"'E's goin' to jump off," shouted Sidney in excitement.

The gunner stood up on tip-toe, curved forward and plunged into the sea.

"'E's mad," said George. "'E's goin' to drown!'

Jimmy was surprised. The tough gunner, who had been so bossy to Miss Cavendish, didn't seem the type to give up and die. Jimmy, Sidney, Keith and George strained over the side of the boat. There was no trace of a swimmer.

The dark waves swirled past. Then, close beside them, sprouted up a head with a scrubby brush of hair. The gunner shook the water off his face and grinned up at their faces.

"Why are you goin' swimmin', mister?" called Sidney.

"Got to keep in practice, keep my swimmin' grand," he gasped.

"Keep yer swimmin' up!" exclaimed George with delight.

"Aye – in case we get torpedoed again. Och!" he called. "It's aye a bonnie day for a swim. Are ye comin' in?"

George roared with laughter.

The gunner kicked his powerful legs and swam alongside them for a while and then he disappeared from sight around the bows of the boat.

Jimmy was amazed. How could the gunner dare to jump into the sea? What would have happened if a wave had dragged him away. They'd never have found him again. He watched anxiously until the shining pink body pulled itself up over the side of the boat, alongside the officers. For the first time Jimmy saw a grin on the face of the men manning the tiller.

"Crikey!" said Sidney.

Jimmy smiled at George with relief. Somehow the sea didn't seem so frightening after all.

"Wish I could swim," said George.

"I can't neither," said Jimmy. "I've only seen the sea once before, on a day trip to Margate, but I bet Keith can – he lives by the sea. Can you swim, Keith?"

Keith nodded thoughtfully.

"You realise the gunner swam round the whole boat and back," he said.

"Yes."

"That means we must be sailing very slowly."

Lunch was the first meal of the day. Jimmy was ravenous. It was bully beef on a hard, crusty biscuit, with one dipper of water. The four boys munched slowly and deliberately, concentrating and not uttering a word.

"So you boys have lost your pocket money, did I hear correctly this morning?"

Baron Wolcinski stumbled over Jimmy's legs as he

returned from his trip to talk to Elizabeth. She had shrieked when he had tried to pull her arm straight but then he had lent his white silk scarf, with its long fringe, to Miss Cavendish to help bind the arm up.

"Yes, mister," said Jimmy.

Baron Wolcinski had taken no notice of the boys until now. Jimmy wondered if he was like Keith, and needed glasses to see them.

"And, if I understand correctly, you've never had pocket money before."

"Well I haven't, mister, nor has Sidney here. Keith's parents couldn't give . . . well they . . ."

"I see," said the Baron, straightening his bow tie. "Then when we land I'll double all the money you boys have lost."

"Double it?"

"Double it!"

Jimmy's breath stopped.

"But Keith and George here, they haven't . . ."

"I'm sure you will decide what's fair," said the Baron.

Jimmy nudged Sidney and grinned at Keith and George. Fair, yes, they could decide what was fair! They would all have the same, just as if George and Keith's parents had given it to them. He couldn't wait for land! He'd be able to buy some sweets for himself and a bar of war-issue chocolate for Mum.

"On one condition," said the Baron. "You boys have got to keep a proper watch for overhead aircraft."

113

★

All afternoon Jimmy's eyes scoured the sky. He strained his ears to hear the drone of aircraft engines, but there was only the pounding of the waves against the boat and the occasional cry of a gull.

Miss Cavendish started telling the stories of the adventures of Bulldog Drummond. The stories weren't much good, but at least it made him think of other things than the boat and the sea and the loneliness.

There was no supper, but as the light of their second day at sea began to fade, the steward passed round holed tins of condensed milk to suck, and a dipperful of water each.

The cold was getting terrible. Miss Cavendish showed them how to rub their legs and feet "to get the blood flowing", but Sidney's stick feet wouldn't get pink again. However much you rubbed them, they remained white with cold. Sidney didn't complain, but his face was as white as his feet and his brown freckles stood out as if they had been sprinkled on with paint. Jimmy and George took hold of one foot each. They rubbed and stroked but they couldn't warm Sidney's icy feet.

Keith sat silently staring. Even he had run out of interesting facts to tell.

Alongside them the Lascar sailors splashed sea water on their hands and heads and even into their mouths, then they spat the water out again.

"Why they doin' that?" said Jimmy. "The steward

said on no account was we to touch sea water – it 'ud make us more thirsty bein' salty."

The Lascars were chanting in unison, rocking gently back and forward.

"They're Muslims," explained Miss Cavendish. "They do that ritual washing to cleanse themselves before they pray, do they not, Father O'Brien?"

"To be sure," he replied.

The priest had been dreadfully sea sick on the first day, and had lain in the bottom of the boat, but he seemed better now. His wan face looked gentle and kind, and not a bit like the face of the devil.

"We should follow the example of the Lascars," said Father O'Brien, "and say the Lord's Prayer together before we sleep,"

"Our Father . . ." he began.

It was comforting reciting together. It made Jimmy feel not so alone and that they would all stand by each other. He must remember to tell Mum that the Papists had the same prayer too. Only Daniel and Jacob remained silently watching.

But at the end of the Lord's Prayer Father O'Brien began to say another prayer which Daniel and Jacob said with him. At least Jimmy thought it was a prayer, but it was in a language as strange as that of the Lascars.

"Father O'Brien has studied Hebrew," said Miss Cavendish with admiration.

"What's that then?" said Sidney, roused from his cold.

"It's the language of the Jews," Keith said. "They're praying to God too."

Jimmy sat back, sunk in thought. What would Mum make of all this?

"We've got to be all right then," he said finally. "We're prayin' to enough Gods in this boat. One of 'em's got to hear us."

Miss Cavendish laughed.

"There's only one God, Jimmy. Chapel people like yourself, Catholics, Muslims, Jews – we all pray to the God of Abraham."

"All prayin' to the same God?" said Jimmy in astonishment. Wonders would never cease!

Right, God, he decided, if You can save us, I'll never cut Sunday school again.

Jimmy thought longingly of all those Sunday afternoons, when, unknown to Mum, he'd gone out, Bible in hand, only to meet Bob and the gang and skive off to the railway sheds. It was a sacrifice, it really was, so he hoped God was listening.

CHAPTER NINE

Jimmy thought back. The hours all seemed the same but he reckoned it was the third night. He huddled under the blanket, next to Sidney, who lay still and quiet, except for sudden bouts of shivering. He pushed his feet over and tried to rub Sidney's freezing toes, but they were cold and stiff, like slabs of ice.

Keith had become quieter and quieter and sat with that dull, death-like expression on his face. It was getting more difficult to get an interesting fact out of him.

"You awake, Jimmy?"

"I can't sleep, George. Sidney is out, but it's like bein' beside a snowman with him beside me."

"Keith's asleep too. Can't tell whether 'e's asleep or awake now. When 'e's awake 'e acts like 'e's asleep."

"You've got to make allowances – he'd lost his mum and dad and a sister the week before he came."

"Never! How'd 'e do that?"

"Bomb. He don't like talkin' about it. I reckon that's the trouble with him. He ain't got no one to go back to."

There was a silence. Jimmy could hear Sidney and Keith's regular breathing, while from George came sharp, irregular little breaths.

"That's no reason to give up," George whispered suddenly. "I ain't got no one wants me neither."

"Don't be stupid! Your mum'll be ever so pleased when you get back safe."

"No. After Dad left, she gave me to the authorities – put me in a 'ome."

"No, that's wrong, George." Jimmy didn't want to believe what he heard. "She sent you to Canada with us."

"It weren't like that . . ." George's voice had dropped to a whisper. Somehow Jimmy knew George had not told any one before, not proud, angry George. Jimmy didn't answer but let him go on and get it off his chest.

". . . the authorities decided I 'ad to go. It don't make much difference to me, one way or t'other."

"Why'd they decide that?" said Jimmy softly.

"Too big, too strong. They said I'd be better off on a farm in Canada, with 'ard work and discipline."

"Trouble, were you then?" Jimmy hardly had to ask. He knew it.

George ignored his question.

"I'll survive this, Jimmy. I'm strong and I don't need no one. Keith's lost his mum and dad and 'e can't survive without them. I'm lucky – I ain't ever had that really, so I don't miss it."

"But I miss me mum and dad. That's why I can hold on, George. You can come and visit. Mum and Dad 'ud like that."

Jimmy wasn't sure Mum and Dad would like George if he was like the old George, but he'd try and explain to them.

"Know why I don't feel too bad, George?"

"You just told me."

"No – I reckon it's because I'm on the hefty side. Sidney here is all skin and bone, but you try pinchin' me arm. It's got a good coverin' on it, it has. It's as good as an extra blanket."

A snort came from George's direction, and Jimmy laughed. At that moment the gunner pushed his way through the sleeping bodies.

"That's right, laugh while ye can," he growled. "Call them young men officers! Why, I've bin at sea close on thirty years and I know more of navigation in my wee finger than they knows in their heads."

The gunner checked the tarpaulin rope, untied a knot with a knowing sigh and retied it.

"And as for these escorts . . . ! Now my wife, she's got a way with bairns, she has. Keeps 'em fit as fleas, and she means business – no nonsense from them, I can tell ye. But I reckon no woman knows how to look after bairns till she has some of her own."

"Gunner Mackenzie, these children are trying to sleep," began Miss Cavendish, "and I'd be grateful . . ."

"What do ye know of bairns and sleep?" he said. Jimmy could hear the enjoyment in his voice. He wasn't being fair, Jimmy knew that, but it was good to listen to a lively voice. "No bairns of your own, no husband . . ."

"Gunner Mackenzie, I insist you leave the children in peace."

The gunner pushed his way back down the boat. ". . . and not likely to find a husband neither," came his parting shot.

The next day, and the day after, seemed to drag on as if they had been in the boat all their lives and would stay there for ever. It was as if time stood still. Day and night passed by with no significance, with nothing to mark them except the brightening and fading light.

Sidney never complained, but whenever his feet were touched now he grimaced with pain. Jimmy worried about him. Sidney was thin at the best of times but now he seemed to be fading away before Jimmy's eyes.

At midday the steward brought the rations.

"Come on, Sidney, eat that biscuit up. It'll make you feel a whole lot better."

"You 'ave it, Jimmy. I can't eat it."

Jimmy stared at the two dry biscuits in his hand. He never thought he could feel starving and not be able to eat, but his mouth and throat were so dry that he couldn't soften the hard crumbs. It was like biting bits of grit.

The thirst was the worst. The dipperful wasn't enough. They were drying out, all of them. If they weren't picked up soon they'd turn into a boatload of dried prunes.

"Tinned salmon today," the steward said.

Jimmy tried to smile but his cracked lips prevented it.

"Look, Sidney, we've got a bit of salmon on the biscuit. It's got a drop of juice in it. It'll make the biscuit soft."

Sidney sucked the biscuit and licked the salmon off, then handed the dry biscuit back.

"You can 'ave it."

Jimmy had managed to eat half of his biscuit, but he put Sidney's and his other half into his pocket.

Just as Jimmy worried himself over Sidney, George bossed over Keith. Keith didn't have much choice. Left to himself Keith seemed to want to give up, not to eat or even drink the water, but George wasn't having any of that.

"If you think yer goin' to get away with it, you ain't. I'm watchin'. You eat that salmon or I'll plaster it somewhere you won't like."

"Salmon," said Keith vaguely. "Sea fish, but spawning grounds in the rivers; can jump up to eleven foot . . ."

"I said *eat it up*! Do you want me to use a bit of this on you?"

George brought his fist up under Keith's chin.

Keith ate. Jimmy didn't think he looked too scared of the fist, or even mind George's bullying.

Miss Cavendish left Jimmy and Keith to get on with it their way. She had her hands full looking after Elizabeth. Elizabeth didn't complain but any time one of the boys jogged her she gave a little yelp of pain. Jimmy didn't like to sit too near her, because, being a bit bulky, he was afraid he'd lean on her arm. She pulled in close to Miss Cavendish, whose other side was cramped by Jacob and Daniel. Jacob and Daniel were nice enough little kids, but they only clung to each other, hand entwined in hand, staring wide-eyed at the bigger boys.

Hour by hour Jimmy's throat was becoming more swollen, so that swallowing became near impossible. His tongue was rough and dry.

On the fourth day heavy rain clouds hung overhead. Jimmy could no longer remember when he had last seen the sun. The swirling, black clouds hung low, meeting the horizon over the waves. Jimmy felt trapped, shut in between dark sea and cloud, the boat a floating prison. There must be a hole in them some- where, a door to let them out of all this sea and sky, there must be . . . he mustn't stop believing.

"Go on – rain!" ordered George.

And as if in answer to his angry demand great sheets of rain swept across the sea and over the boat. The boys kept their mouths open although it was dreadful how little they could catch, but at least it wet their rough tongues and throats.

The rain had passed and it grew colder again. Suddenly Jimmy was stung by icy pinpricks. On his navy life jacket lay little balls of ice.

"It's hail, it is! Lick 'em, Sidney – lick 'em with your tongue!"

The boat awoke with commotion. The steward stumbled over bodies, handing out empty tins cans to hold.

Keith, who sat there quietly and soberly, was given an empty salmon tin. As soon as the steward had turned, George grabbed it off him.

"Give it me. We've got to do this properly, we 'ave."

He pushed away Keith's limp hand and held the tin out over the side of the boat. The hailstones pinged against the side of the tin and, to Jimmy's horror, jump straight out again as soon as they landed.

"It's no good," muttered Keith. "It's the velocity. They're coming down with too much force."

George yelled with frustration as the hailstones bounced out.

"Clever, ain't you," George spat out with fury. "Think yer've got an answer for everythin'. If we all knew as much as you, we 'ud never do nothin."

Keith didn't seem to mind George's anger. His mouth stretched and Jimmy wasn't sure if he detected a smile.

With ceremony George passed round the tin. It was as good as empty but Jimmy pretended to sip.

★

"Two of you lads give me a hand?" The slight figure of Petty Officer Hamilton dragged out the tarpaulin from under their seat.

George leapt up. Elizabeth let out a yelp of pain. George looked embarrassed but ignored her.

Jimmy stared across the gap at Elizabeth. She looked awful – white and tired and she still had that ridiculous pink ribbon hanging down her hair. She stared blankly back. Jimmy wanted to say something to her – she looked so unhappy – but he couldn't find the words. He remembered her posh voice as she had talked to her mother above his head on the first-class deck, but she had wanted to play, like the other children. She had been lonely . . .

"Still hurtin', is it?"

Elizabeth nodded, as if she couldn't trust herself to speak.

"We'll be gettin' there soon."

She stared blankly at Jimmy.

"Ireland, you know. That's where we're headin'. I expect you've bin there."

She nodded.

"On yer grandad's yacht, I bet. Tell 'im he can take me as cabin boy next time. By the time we get out of this, I'll know all about the sea, I will."

Elizabeth smiled. For a brief moment Jimmy forgot the cold. He looked away, feeling his face flush with warmth.

"I'll help," he called to George and Petty Officer Hamilton, who were struggling with the tarpaulin.

"No you won't," George shoved Jimmy roughly away. He grabbed Keith and hauled him to his feet. "I've got this lazy lout to 'elp me. Now get a move on, Keith, before I get me knee to you."

Keith seemed to wake up as he rose.

"What are we going to do with the tarpaulin?" he asked Petty Officer Hamilton with a flicker of interest.

"There's more rain coming, lads. If we can get this tarpaulin horizontal round the mast and sag it into a bowl shape, we might get a bit of water."

"Like an overhead storage tank?" suggested Keith.

"Exactly!"

The rain came. Jimmy listened to the marvellous sound of rain drumming on the canvas. After a while the sound turned into plops as the rain fell on the gathering pool of water. He was so thirsty! More thirsty than he had ever been in his life.

When the rain had stopped the steward approached the sagging tarpaulin with the dipper in his hand. Jimmy's eyes followed his every move as he filled the dipper and raised it to his lips.

The steward smacked his lips, emptied the dipper and tried again. Slowly he carried the dipper back to the stern and handed it to Lieutenant Ingram. Lieutenant Ingram sipped, paused and passed it to the chief steward. Angry murmurs rose from the Lascars and the boys watched in agony.

125

Jimmy couldn't believe it . . . The plump, kindly steward, in full view of all the boat, emptied the dipper over the side. Jimmy was in torment.

The gunner stomped down the boat, barging over everyone's feet without so much as a glance or apology. He untied the tarpaulin and the pitiful pool of water fell in the boat. Jimmy joined George and the Lascars, desperately scrabbling to scoop up water from the floor.

"Leave it!" shouted the gunner. "Fat lot of use that was – mad idea. Now, if anyone had asked me . . ."

"Why can't we drink it, mister?" Jimmy called.

"It's salt, that's why. It isni' better than the sea."

"Salt?"

"Yes. It would send us mad, kill us. Should have thought of it, those young fools. Stands to reason that a tarpaulin that covers a boat is salty."

Jimmy staggered back, aching with disappointment. Even George looked downcast.

"He's quite right," said Keith suddenly. "It's been continually wetted with sea spray, which has evaporated and left the salt. The canvas is probably impregnated with salt and makes the rainwater . . ."

"Shut up, can't you," said George. "No, on second thoughts tell me somethin' – anyone seen Ireland?"

"Don't be funny," groaned Jimmy.

"We've got time, then, for a bit of explainin' " said George, looking round with grim determination in his eyes. "You tell us, Keith."

Jimmy was glad of Keith's droning voice. He wasn't

126

listening. He bet none of them was listening, but at least they could hide behind Keith's voice, locked in their own misery.

They did not sleep that night. The worst storm they had yet faced broke over them. The freezing wind bit at Jimmy's cheeks so that he huddled his icy face down into his sodden life jacket. His pyjamas were soaked too, and he shivered inside the clinging wet legs. Someone out there, behind the clouds, under the waves, had it in for them. In the shrieking wind he heard laughter, screaming, evil laughter.

The boat pitched and heaved, throwing them continually about and around, tumbling on each other. Jimmy tried to cushion Sidney's flaying limbs with his own legs. He'd always had solid legs, but they were stocky and strong legs. Now they seemed to register every bruise. Jimmy put his hand down and felt his calves. Yes, he was convinced. There was a lot less of him than he remembered.

"George," Jimmy yelled across Sidney, "someone out there don't like us. I reckon they've got it in for us."

"Good!" yelled George. "I like a fight. We'll beat 'em, Jimmy, you see. No one's ever beaten me yet."

Jimmy stuck up his thumb. Sidney saw and slowly put his up too.

"All right, Sidney?"

"Fine . . . I'm fine," whispered Sidney. "We'll get

'em . . .", and he sank back, his head against Jimmy's shoulder.

It was getting difficult to talk, their throats were so dry.

Jimmy watched the gunner, four Lascars, Petty Officer Hamilton and even at times Baron Wolcinski, his black and bedraggled Homburg hat crammed low over his face, take turns at the handles. In the stern, Lieutenant Ingram and the chief steward struggled to hold the tiller on course.

It was difficult keeping the sail down. The gunner tied two of its corners to the awning, while six Lascars wrestled all night with it, trying to hold it in the boat. Sometimes they were driven to lying on top of it with legs and arms dangling over the sides.

Several times Jimmy was convinced they were finished. Once a grey wave came towards them, so huge he thought it was one of the engine sheds from home, bombed, crashing down on top of them, but it filled the boat with spray and water, not bricks and mortar. Every man was busy, bailing out with buckets and tins, anything that could be found. But the waves came again and again, relentless in their attack.

Jimmy felt dreadfully sick but he had nothing inside him to vomit.

"Sidney?" he whispered.

There was silence before Sidney answered, as if it was a huge effort, "What . . . do you . . . want?"

"You got the lucky shrapnel safe?"

"Yeah."

"We'll be all right then."

The next day, when dawn broke, the storm died. Jimmy sat alongside Sidney, Keith and George, all of them dozing with exhaustion. They were wet and cold and Sidney's toes had turned a strange mottled colour.

"Wake up – it's Sunday!"

Jimmy opened his eyes to see the smiling chief steward, his plump face leaner and shadowed with the beginnings of a dark beard. Behind the steward sat Father O'Brien, pale and thin, his mouth moving until he made a funny sign, crossing himself.

"Sunday . . . ?"

"You can say your prayers later," smiled the steward. "We've got all day."

Mum would be going to morning chapel. Was she praying for him? If she was, he could give it a miss. He was so tired, too tired to pray and Mum prayed enough. Surely she'd be praying for both of them.

"Sunday lunch – and I've got something special."

Jimmy stared.

It was a dry biscuit, but on it lay a shining, moist, yellow segment of canned peach. Carefully he took it, cradling it in his hand. It smelt of heaven and home and special treats for Sunday tea.

"Here, Sidney, open yer mouth."

Sidney opened his eyes and his mouth. Then he quickly shut his mouth again.

"What is it? I don't want no more of them biscuits
. . . Crikey! Where'd you get that?"

Sidney let Jimmy tip the sweet slice of peach into his
mouth. His tongue, dry as a lizard's licked every drop
of sugary juice off his lips.

Jimmy took his biscuit from the steward. Like Sidney
he couldn't eat the biscuit, but the segment of peach,
all soft and cool, slithered into his dry mouth and
slipped down his tight throat.

Then the steward took a dipperful of water for each
of them and poured the water into an empty condensed
milk tin. Every eye in the boat was on him as he added
a little peach juice to each portion. Nothing, in all
Jimmy's life, had tasted or smelt so delicious.

He sat back, dreaming of fruit and sunshine, remem-
bering the last time he had tasted an orange, the only
one he had had since the war started. He found he
could smell it and taste it and see it as if it were there in
his hand. He held up his hand to have a closer look, but
his eyes wouldn't focus. They stared past, away into the
distance, to the horizon, to a speck that smudged the
otherwise straight line.

Jimmy stared, then struggled to his feet.

"You should tell us when yer gettin' up," grumbled
George. "I don't like bein' shoved and pushed."

"Look!" cried Jimmy, blinking to test his eyes.

"Seen a ghost?" teased George.

Jimmy raised his hand and pointed, "Look! Can't
you see it . . . ?"

130

CHAPTER TEN

Voices stopped. The men at the handles rested and stared as word passed along the boat. The Lascar seamen craned over the side, while the officers in the stern stood motionless, like a group of shabby statues.

Jimmy peered. It was a ship – he couldn't be wrong. The dot was gradually getting bigger, and yes – he was sure – a wisp floated up from the dot, pale against the dark storm clouds gathering behind it. A wisp of smoke, from the mouth of a little stick. It was the funnel. You could see it clearly now – the funnel of a steamer.

"Blimey!" whispered Sidney.

The Lascars erupted in excited shouts. The officers, still unable to take their eyes off the ship, had grins stretching across their faces. Miss Cavendish curled her arms around Elizabeth on one side, and Daniel and Jacob on the other, and hugged them. Tears poured down Elizabeth's face, while Baron Wolcinski took off his black hat and waved it in the air.

"Well done, boy," he shouted at Jimmy. "I'll triple your money!"

Triple – that was three times. Phew! Jimmy let out a

whoop, closely followed by a blood-curdling war cry from George.

As for Keith, he couldn't stop gabbling. "It won't be a passenger liner – I can't see – is it a stubby shape? If the gun turrets are missing it won't be a destroyer either. It could be a freighter, sailing outside a convoy, from a neutral country . . ."

"I don't care what it is," shouted George. "As long as it's a boat."

"How about a bath tub then?" said Jimmy.

"Suits me," said George. "As long as it floats."

Jimmy turned and smiled at Miss Cavendish. She'd been so good and patient with them. She was a quiet lady, but now Jimmy came to think of it she couldn't have had much sleep, looking after all of them. Jimmy had quite a few aunties, but he reckoned if Miss Cavendish had been one, she'd have been his favourite.

Tears were still dripping down Elizabeth's nose and on to her life jacket.

"What's up then?" said Jimmy.

He couldn't bear tears. There'd been too much crying in his house when his sister had died.

It only seemed to make her worse. Jimmy leant over and patted her on the head. His little sister had liked that when she cried.

"I'm . . . so . . . happy," Elizabeth choked out.

She pulled herself up and Jimmy felt a wet, snivelling kiss land on his cheek. He reddened and quickly wiped it off with his sleeve, looking away so that his mates wouldn't see. They were all gazing out at the dot which was now clearly ship-shaped. Jimmy squeezed in beside Sidney.

"Soppy lot, aren't they?" Sidney whispered.

"Who?"

"Girls."

The boat teemed with action. Petty Officer Hamilton leapt from gap to gap down the boat.

"Anyone got that handkerchief you kids were washing with? We need a flag for the mast, to make sure they see us."

The thought that they might not be seen created panic in the boat.

"But no one will see a handkerchief," said Baron Wolcinski. "Take my silk scarf, the one round the girl's arm."

"Good idea, sir!" said the petty officer.

"Elizabeth needs it," protested Miss Cavendish. "Her arm is setting; we can't disturb the bones."

"But we must have something white," persisted the petty officer with annoyance. "They'll only see something white against the dark sea and sky."

"I know," said Miss Cavendish quietly.

Jimmy watched as she put her hand inside her blouse. She struggled and tugged at something on her shoulder until it snapped. Then she attacked the other shoulder and Jimmy heard a distinct tear. She stood up and put her hand up under her skirt. Jimmy knew he shouldn't watch, but he and all the boys couldn't take their eyes off this fascinating scene. With a couple of tugs down came a silky petticoat, a bit like Mum's best pink petticoat he'd seen hanging on the line, except this one was white.

"Jolly good!" boomed Baron Wolcinski. "Well done."

Petty Officer Hamilton grinned sheepishly and bore the white petticoat to the mast. Tearing a hole in it, he attached it to a rope and hauled it to the top. There it flapped and whipped, a white pennant in the rising wind.

The freighter steamed across their path. It had no flags to identify it and it didn't seem to have seen them.

Everyone stood and yelled and waved. Sidney couldn't stand on his mottled feet, but he waved feebly by Jimmy's side.

"Wave!" screamed George. "Go on – wave everyone."

"What you think we're doin'," said Jimmy anxiously. "Playin' tiddly winks?"

The uproar and waving in the boat was like a long-dormant volcano, erupting at last. The gunner was signalling with semaphore flags in the stern, while the boat was well under sail with a good breeze carrying them rapidly towards the freighter.

The ship could be seen clearly now. Broad and squat, she sat low in the water, her hull a dirty beige colour. She seemed to slow, come to a halt, and then change direction and proceed in a straight line towards them.

"They've seen us!" called Jimmy. "We'll meet again, don't know where, don't know when!" he sang lustily.

"But I know we'll meet again some sunny day . . . !" caterwauled George in reply.

"Come on, Keith, sing!" George gave Keith's arm a pinch.

Sidney couldn't sing, but Jimmy waved his arms to conduct the others, with Jacob and Daniel grinning and even Elizabeth joining.

"Keep smilin' thro' just like you always do,

Till the blue skies drive the dark clouds far a . . ."

The freighter had slowed down. Close to, Jimmy could see the beige paint was peeling on her battered hull, revealing the dirty white she must once have been. Sailors swarmed on the deck, rushing to peer down over the railings.

Petty Officer Hamilton edged back along the boat.

"Message from Lieutenant Ingram – prepare to disembark. They'll be throwing a line down to us soon."

"How will we get on?" asked Jimmy. The ship might not be a big freighter, but it was enormous compared with them.

"They'll have rope ladders," explained Keith. "They'll be getting them out now."

"How far away are we then?" said George.

Keith narrowed his eyes and squinted. "A quarter of a mile, I would guess. I can't see them properly yet."

"Hope they stop in time," said Jimmy. He didn't like the idea of being run down.

As he spoke the ship stopped, and slowly, gradually turned until she was broadside on. The sailors on deck had disappeared.

The gunner stamped down the boat. Together with three Lascar crewmen, he pulled down the tarpaulin awning and folded it up.

"Get the stanchions out of the way," he shouted. "We canni' have the bairns' legs crushed between the stanchions and the ship's side."

The men struggled to pull the heavy iron bars, which had supported the awning, out of their sockets.

"Chuck 'em over," grinned the gunner. "Get rid of 'em. We won't be needing them again."

The Lascars threw one over and it sank without trace under the hurling waves. It was getting rough again and the dark seas were rising. Beyond the steamer, black, turbulent clouds were massing on the horizon.

The gunner helped the Lascars with the second stanchion. The third was stuck but even the Baron joined them, full of sudden energy and enthusiasm as they heaved the heavy iron out of the socket and chucked it over into the sea.

They were pulling on the last stanchion when the gunner stopped, looked over at the ship and stood up. He put his hand out in a gesture to stop the other men.

Then he let out such a stream of obscenity and blasphemy that it held the boys chilled and spellbound.

Jimmy followed the gunner's gaze. He could see the faces of several sailors, busy again on the deck, their dark clothes conspicuous against the beige paintwork. But the dark shapes were moving away now, becoming smaller rather than larger, and less distinct.

"No . . . !" said Jimmy. "No . . . ! No . . . ! No!"

"The bastards," muttered George. "I'll kill 'em!"

"What they doin', Jimmy?" muttered Sidney. "What's goin' on?"

"Going on!" yelled the gunner. "They're leaving us that's what!"

That night Jimmy gave up hope – almost. George was beside him, teeth gritted, hissing into his ear.

"We'll manage without 'em. You see. We'll get to Ireland without 'em . . . We don't need 'em."

"I won't get no triple pocket money now."

"Bastards!"

"Why'd they leave us, George?"

"Dunno – the bastards!"

Jimmy sank back. They ignored each other's eyes, unable to face the despair Jimmy felt like a heavy smog enveloping them.

No one spoke, except George. He muttered on, lashing himself into a fury. Jimmy had never seen George so angry. George reminded him of a smouldering fire, like the one in the parlour on Sunday. It took ages to light, because the parlour was damp. Dad used the bellows, till slowly, slowly he conjured up flames which sent a faint, flickering warmth into the room. By the time they went to bed the room was at last warm and the fire flaming.

Jimmy was in the parlour, cold and damp. He could feel a flicker of flame from George's fire, but could George blaze enough to warm them all?

"Why'd they leave us?" he murmured again to himself.

"They might have thought we were a trap," came Keith's gloomy voice. "The sailors in Southampton say that a U-boat can disguise its tower when it surfaces, by sticking a lifeboat on it."

"You mean they thought we was the top of a U-boat?"

"They could have . . ."

Now that three of the four stanchions supporting the awning had gone, the tarpaulin was forced down lower over their heads. Beneath it they had to sit with heads bent and move around in a crouch.

The gunner came to check. He never mentioned losing the stanchions overboard, but he tried, in vain, to raise the tarpaulin. Jimmy stared up at the square bullet of a man.

"What's the matter with all of ye?" the gunner yelled. "Look as if it's the end of the world. Och, it isni'! She didni' pick us up, but that's ni' the sort of thing to make a fuss about. It's good news, see – we must be in the shipping lanes. There'll be plenty more ships passing tomorrow to pick us up."

"Shipping lanes?" muttered Keith. "If we're in the shipping lanes, that will be the one to Canada. I don't see how we can be in the right direction for Ireland. Wouldn't we pass to the north of Ireland . . . ?

"What a clever wee sailor we have here," said the gunner in disgust. "I've got enough of them in the stern. That young whippet of a petty officer, younger than my eldest he is, thinking he knows all about navigation. I tell ye I've been at sea close on thirty years and I –"

"I'm sure we're getting closer to Ireland," interrupted Miss Cavendish. She looked nervously at the terrified faces of Jacob and Daniel at her side.

"Ye can talk, missus!" exclaimed the gunner. "Why are ye ni' keeping their spirits up? I dinni' ken what ye escorts are on this job for. My wife could do a better job standing on her hands than what's going on here. How about it, laddies, how about another of those adventures of Captain Drummond?"

Jimmy and George both shouted: "Yes!"

Keith looked expectant and even Sidney tried to listen.

Miss Cavendish wearily settled the little boys on her right and with effort began to tell of how the fearless hero, Bulldog Drummond, infiltrated single-handed through enemy lines to an assignation with a secret agent, who never turned up . . . It was a pathetic story

139

really. Miss Cavendish was the loveliest lady Jimmy had met in a long time, but she was a rotten storyteller. But it didn't matter. He wanted to forget himself, forget where they were, forget the ship that had abandoned him, so Jimmy followed Bulldog Drummond, trying to imagine him sneaking through some place called the Black Forest.

The story didn't end, but faded away in the dark and the shrieking of the wind. The storm had arrived with full force.

Jimmy woke. His feet and legs were numb. It was dark, the moon hidden by swirling black storm clouds. The boat was tossed and spun on the waves. It would be smashed to pieces any minute by a towering wave and they would be gone without a trace.

"Jimmy."

"You awake, Sidney?"

"We ain't goin' to make it, Jimmy."

"It'll all come right," Jimmy answered dully and without conviction.

"Do you believe in devils, Jimmy?"

"Well . . . I ain't seen one, but we had a preacher at our chapel and he went on and on about the devil."

"There's more than one, Jimmy. They're devils out there and they're tryin' to get us."

They listened to the shrieking wind. Jimmy could hear them now, he could hear their evil voices and their rejoicing over the despair in the boat. They were in the wind and in the waves that bore them to the top of dizzying waves and then crashed them down into troughs, imprisoned by solid walls of water.

But again and again the wind suddenly dropped. Just when Jimmy was most terrified and thought they were done for, the waves slid back and failed to crush them.

"It ain't just devils out there, Sidney," whispered Jimmy in one of the brief interludes when a wave had fallen back as it was about to crash over them. "I reckon there's someone tryin' to hold them back."

All night it continued. They were like a handful of fragile marbles caught in some deadly game. One moment they were in the hands of death and the next they were grabbed back from the grip of the devils.

Jimmy scarcely noticed the passage of night to dawn. The sky merely became grey, but the storm raged on.

"Hands to handles," came the faint shout, passed down the boat.

A Lascar swayed unsteadily forward to replace an exhausted man at the handles. No one else moved.

"Hands to handles," came the cry again.

In the early days all the men had rushed to do their share on the handles. Now Jimmy could see that they were as weak and exhausted as himself. Only the gunner had lost none of his energy. Every day he had dived overboard for his swim around the boat, a swim that seemed to put new life in him. Now he pushed his way down the boat, roughly grabbing men by the shoulders and pushing them towards the handles.

"It won't get us far in these heavy seas," said Keith suddenly with gloom.

"Why don't they give over till it gets calmer?" said Jimmy. "They're only wearin' themselves out. If they wait till it's calmer we can get somewhere."

"They've got to keep going. It's not just to move us forward – it keeps the boat steady."

"I'm goin' to give it a go," said George suddenly, as he pulled himself to his feet.

"Ye, laddie?" said the gunner. "Och, why not! Ye's a big lad. That's the sort of man I like to see!"

Jimmy swelled with pride for George as he watched him barge his way down the boat, into place on one of the handles. He nudged Sidney and grinned, while Keith blinked, trying to focus on George. George was their mate, one of them, and it was as if he was working the handles for them all.

Some of the men watched with astonishment until, one by one, four more men hauled themselves up and took the places of the exhausted men on the handles. George didn't last too long. He was strong, but not as strong as a man, and he was weakened by hunger and lack of sleep, but Jimmy saw that all the boat had watched him and been stirred by his effort.

They kept up a slow pace in the heavy seas but, after the noontime rations, when every eye had watched the slightest gesture of the chief steward as he measured out the water, Jimmy felt more heartened.

"A slow but steady pace," Miss Cávendish smiled encouragingly at the boys. "We must be getting close to land soon."

"Six days at sea – we must be very close to land now," said Baron Wolcinski loudly.

"Hear that, Sidney?" said Jimmy. "Should be land soon. We've just got to hold on that bit . . ."

Jimmy was worried. This morning he couldn't even get a smile out of Sidney.

George sat there with a determined grin on his face.

"See – you got it wrong, Keith," he announced triumphantly. "There's land comin' and I bet it'll be Ireland."

"Let us pray that God will guide us," said Father O'Brien solemnly.

"I dunno!" whispered George. "Between Keith's book knowledge and Father O'Brien handin' the lot over to God, I ain't got much confidence in neither of 'em."

Jimmy giggled.

"Keith's got it wrong about the shipping lane not passin' by Ireland," George's whisper grew louder, "and 'ow can Father O'Brien be sure that God knows the way to Ireland? God's used to bein' up there lookin' down, not arrivin' in a lifeboat."

Jimmy laughed. George was wicked but Jimmy loved it. Even Keith smiled. They weren't sure if

Father O'Brien heard, but he seemed to be looking up to heaven expectantly.

"I tell you, Jimmy, there ain't anyone you can count on but yerself. It's no good relyin' on anyone else."

" 'Cept us George – you can rely on us," said Jimmy stoutly. "We're your mates."

George stared at Jimmy and lapsed into thought.

"Land!"

"Land?"

It was well on in the afternoon. Jimmy was sitting in a stupor, staring at the sullen sea.

"Land, Jimmy!" shouted George. "I told yer! Didn't I tell yer?"

"Thank the Lord!" cried Father O'Brien.

Jimmy gazed dully to the horizon. The sky was already beginning to darken. He couldn't see anything.

"I can't see any land," announced Keith suspiciously.

"Course you can't," shouted George. "You ain't got yer glasses on."

Jimmy strained his eyes and concentrated.

"It's on the horizon," said Miss Cavendish, her quiet voice tense with excitement. "Look, Elizabeth, can you see the line of low hills on the horizon?"

Suddenly Jimmy saw it. It had been there all along but he hadn't been able to make sense of it. Now he could see the hills and the strip of shore in front of them. It was land.

As if in response to their discovery a strong, steady

144

breeze blew, carrying them smoothly forward under sail. The wild gusts of the storm had blown themselves out and the boat was no longer thrown from side to side by the waves.

"Is it Ireland?" shouted Jimmy.

"Sure to be," said George.

"I'm not convinced . . ." began Keith.

"Shut up, Keith!" said George.

Keith persisted. "It could be Scotland – if we are as far north as I suspect. It could even be the Shetland Islands. It depends on whether we took a north-easterly course, or a north-north-east course, so . . ."

The sun was sinking. The clouds were breaking up after the storm and the setting sun rimmed their edges with glowing light. Would they make it before nightfall? Jimmy dreaded another night at sea, each night was getting worse than the last.

The land didn't seem to get any closer in the fading light.

"But the horizon always looks closer than it really is," explained Miss Cavendish cheerfully.

Jimmy stared and stared as the sails held taut and the boat sped on, until twilight blended the land into the same grey as the sky, and then the land's outline disappeared altogether in the darkness.

"We'll be there before mornin'," said Sidney to no one in particular.

Someone edged his way down the boat and stopped at the mast.

"What's he doin'?" said Jimmy.

"He's puttin' somethin' up the mast," said George.

They watched as a yellow light flared up the mast-head. It shot down beams to encircle the slight figure of Petty Officer Hamilton in his ragged naval uniform.

"What's that for, mister?" called George.

"It's a flare. We don't want any shipping ramming us in the night," called back the petty officer. "And it's to inform the coastguards that we're out here."

The pool of light in the middle of the boat was comforting in the blackness. Out there in the dark there were ships and land, thought Jimmy, and the devils would be gone for ever.

CHAPTER ELEVEN

Keith fell asleep quickly, as if it made little difference to him whether he landed or not. George remained upright, expectant, peering into the darkness.

"We must be there soon – we must be," he muttered.

Jimmy was worried about Sidney. He wouldn't speak and didn't seem to take in that they were about to reach land. It was obvious that he needed proper help now, more than he, Jimmy, could give. Thank God they would be landed by morning.

Jimmy dozed off, but was woken by sudden shouting from Sidney. He gabbled on about Babs and his mum, but he didn't seem to be making any sense.

"Hang on, Sid," said Jimmy. "We're almost there."

"It's me feet," screamed Sidney. "They 'urt somethin' terrible."

Jimmy knew they must be agonising. Sidney, despite the dreadful state he was in, had never complained before. Miss Cavendish, a worried frown on her face, leant over and began massaging his foot.

"I'll do the other one, miss," Jimmy volunteered.

"Would you, Jimmy?" said Miss Cavendish in a cracked voice.

Jimmy held the frozen foot between his hands and energetically rubbed it. His own feet were freezing too, but nothing like Sidney's. Despite their rubbing, Sidney's feet remained swollen, stiff blocks of ice. Miss Cavendish untied the strings of her life jacket.

"Hold this for me, Jimmy."

She took off her smart suit jacket and wrapped it round Sidney's feet and then rearranged the blanket on top.

Jimmy felt her shivering in her thin blouse, as she put her life jacket back on. He reckoned she wouldn't be decent if she gave away any more clothes.

Jimmy could feel bruises all over his body. They had been squeezed in so tight for so long now, thrown around and buffeted by the waves. He knew he was thinner – a lot thinner. Sometimes he slipped his hands under his life jacket to warm them, and he could feel the bony ridges of his ribs. And he had to keep tightening the cord of his pyjama trousers to stop them falling down.

His thoughts were interrupted by a painful pinch on the arm.

"Look, Jimmy! Look at them lights!"

George tugged on Jimmy's arm. Had they got there at last? Jimmy saw golden light dancing in front of his eyes.

"Wake up, Keith!" George shook Keith awake. "There's lights out there. It's gotta be land."

Keith opened his eyes and surveyed the dark water.

A belt of flickering light was flashing over the water, so that the fish, swimming beside the boat, glinted like fluid silver and gold.

Keith silently surveyed the sea.

"No . . . Those aren't shore lights," he said.

"Course they are!" shouted George. He stared out over the flickering sea. "Or it's a ship – it must be."

"It's phosphorescence," said Keith insistently.

"Fosferwhat?" said George. "That's light out there, that is. I'm not stupid."

"Yes, phosphorescence is a sort of light," said Keith patiently. "But it's part of a chemical reaction in the sea – it's not from the shore."

"You should shut up if you ain't got anythin' encouragin' to say," said George angrily.

"You asked – "

"Aw – forget it!"

Jimmy woke to the sound of booms and distant cracks and rumbles. For a moment he thought he was in the tube station, listening to an overhead bombing raid.

He sat up. George was wide awake. Sidney opened his eyes blankly.

"That's guns and bombs, George."

Keith was awake in a flash.

"Where? I can't see . . . Tell me, Jimmy, are they coming for us?"

Keith started shaking uncontrollably.

Jimmy leant across Sidney to hold on to Keith, but

George already had his arms tight round him.

"Stop that shakin', do you hear? I'm not havin' it,"
George ordered. "Do you think I'm goin' to let any
bombs get me? Do you think I am? Come on – answer
me!"

Keith contined to shudder.

"No," he said, his teeth chattering.

"Course they're not, stupid! Even a dummy can see
you're next to me, so is a bomb going to get you?"

Keith didn't answer.

"Come on, clever clogs, tell me."

"No."

"What are you worried about then? Sidney's got the
lucky shrapnel, ain't you, Sidney?"

Sidney grunted.

Ahead of the boat, Jimmy glimpsed flashes of light,
different from the phosphorescence. They were a long
way away and lit up the horizon like a lightning flash.
But it wasn't lightning. Lightning came from the sky
down, not from the sea up. If there was bombing and
fighting out there, Jimmy knew one thing . . .

"Keith's right, you know," he shouted with excitement. "That's bombin', that is, and Ireland isn't at war,
so it's got to be Scotland."

As the sky paled to grey they all kept their eyes fixed
on the eastern horizon. The sky became lighter, flatter
and the horizon was completely empty. The flat grey
sky was clear of yesterday's dark clouds, and with the
clouds, the land had vanished.

They sat in silence not talking. Jimmy's mind wouldn't work. All he knew was that the clouds had looked so like land, they had so much wanted it to be land . . . He tried to keep it going by working out how long they'd been in the lifeboat. He reckoned it was a week now. How long could you survive like this? How much water had the chief steward left? The thirst was unbearable. He thought of water all the time.

Two Lascars laid one of their men gently in the bottom of the boat, across their feet. The man didn't seem to be able to sit upright any longer.

In the middle of the day the chief steward brought round the water. Jimmy watched him working his way down the boat, concentrating on pouring each precious drop. The friendly chief steward never smiled at the children now, but seemed to avoid looking them in the eye.

Most of the day they sat quiet, without talking. There was nothing new to say any more and talking hurt too much and was too much effort.

That evening Miss Cavendish tried another instalment of Captain Drummond, but her voice was hoarse and she seemed to forget what she had said from one minute to the next.

That night Jimmy and Miss Cavendish tried to rub Sidney's legs but he couldn't bear them to be touched.

"Leave 'em," he shouted.

The moonlight was silvery and eerie overhead.

Shadows from the rigging threw dark lines across the boat.

"It's prison," said Sidney frantically. "Jimmy, we's in prison."

Jimmy roused himself from his semi-sleep. "Course it's not, Sidney."

"It is. We're bad, Jimmy. They've put us in prison. Look – them bars – you see them?"

"That's not bars, Sidney. That's the shadows of the rigging, it's the – "

"Let me out! We got to get out. They got us locked up – "

"It's all right, Sidney. We're goin' to get out. Just hold on."

"I'm goin' mad, I'm goin' mad, Jimmy – I know I'm goin' mad."

The thin, dark shadow of Petty Officer Hamilton, his face pale and ghostlike, loomed out of the dark.

"Miss Cavendish, keep that boy quiet!"

Miss Cavendish roused herself. She seemed hardly aware herself of what was going on.

"Yes . . . yes," she muttered vaguely.

"Lieutenant Ingram has sent me down. He wants the boys quiet. There's to be no panic in the boat. Panic is dangerous in our situation, Miss Cavendish. It could spread."

By now all the boys were awake.

"Let me see the boy," came the quiet voice of Father O'Brien. He bent over Sidney and smoothed back the hair from his terrified face. "This boy is dying of thirst – he has to have water," said the priest firmly. "Tell the chief steward, the boy must have an extra dipperful if we are to save him."

Petty Officer Hamilton hesitated, as if unsure what to do. Without a word he turned and stumbled back to the stern. A few minutes later he reappeared beside them, and from under his jacket produced the dipper. As he lowered it carefully to Sidney, who lay propped in Father O'Brien's arms, Jimmy saw the barest covering of water shimmer in the bottom of the dipper. It could hardly have been more than a spoonful.

"We can't do this again," whispered Petty Officer Hamilton. "The steward said we must all be treated equally. If the rest of the boat discover someone is having preferential treatment, we'll have a mutiny on our hands. Lieutenant Ingram says discipline must be maintained at all cost."

When the petty officer had left, Father O'Brien held Sidney cradled in his arms. He was muttering over him in another of those strange languages.

"What's he up to, George?" said Jimmy with an effort.

"Dunno."

"It's Latin," said Keith slowly. "They're the prayers for the dying."

The boys sat still and shocked.

"Water? Where's the water!" came a sudden cry from Sidney. "Water! Water!" he screamed out again.

Muttering flickered round the boat, followed by a crashing and blundering as the dark stocky outline of the gunner made its way down the boat.

"What's this racket then? The bairn not being cared for, it wouldni' surprise me!"

The gunner cast a dismissive look at Miss Cavendish and Father O'Brien.

"Water!" Sidney croaked.

"Water?" repeated the gunner. "Och – is that all it is? Of course ye want water, we all do. We'll get our water in the morning."

"Water . . . water . . . water," cried Sidney piteously.

This wasn't the Sidney Jimmy knew. This was some terrible, wretched being.

"Now ye forget about water," the gunner ordered. "We'll have gallons of water as soon as we're picked up, and we're going to be picked up before ye can say Jock Mackenzie. Water! Is that all that's bothering ye. I wouldni' have bothered coming down the boat if I'd a known it was just water."

Sidney seemed to calm under the gunner's stern orders, lulled by his harsh but confident voice.

"My feet are cold," he whispered weakly.

"Feet! Well, why didni' ye tell me? I don't know . . . What are these escorts up to? Are ye not being properly looked after?"

He roughly pulled off the jacket Miss Cavendish had bound round Sidney's feet and rearranged it.

"Better?"

"They're still cold."

The gunner grunted and made off back down the boat. He soon reappeared, carrying a torn naval jacket. Jimmy recognised it as the one Petty Officer Hamilton wore over his life jacket.

Clumsily the gunner pulled the coat round Sidney's legs.

"Are your feet warmer now?"

"They're cold," came the whisper from Sidney.

"Nay, they're not," said the gunner firmly. "They're wrapped up proper now, and they'll be as warm as toast in a jiffy. Now, are your feet warm?"

"My feet . . ."

"I'll not hear another sound out of ye till the morning," said the gunner fiercely. "None of this fussing and yelling out. Now – are your feet warm?"

"Yes," said Sidney feebly.

"Then ye'll be fine till the morning."

"Yes."

"I don't know – proper care he needs, not all this praying nonsense, and women who've never even had a bairn of their own to learn from. Beats me how these escorts . . ." And his muttering faded down the boat.

Jimmy smiled. He lay squeezed up beside Sidney and put his hand out to let him know he was there.

Sidney did not scream again and Jimmy slept.

CHAPTER TWELVE

Jimmy was at home, not in the damp parlour, nor his cold bedroom, but in the warm, cosy kitchen. His mother had stoked the fire in the range and he could feel its heat toasting his icy feet and soothing his chapped face. After the horrors of the night the warmth enveloped him like a comforting blanket and he dozed peacefully, as he had never managed before in the boat.

"Jimmy! Come on, wake up!"

Something was gripping Jimmy's arm and shaking it. His arm was thin now and it hurt, but he didn't want to wake up. He wanted to be left – warm and peaceful for every moment he could snatch.

" 'Ave a look, Jimmy!"

Jimmy irritably forced his eyes open. There was George, his face enveloped in a golden glow like the picture of the angel in Mum's Bible, spoilt only by the devilish grin on his face and his vice-like grip on Sidney's arm.

"Look! Not bad, eh, Jimmy."

Jimmy heaved himself up. He couldn't believe his eyes. An orange-yellow sun hung above the misty horizon ahead of them. Beneath it the sea lay calm and deep blue, sparkling with white and silver ripples when the breeze stirred its smooth surface.

This was how the sea looked in picture postcards. Jimmy had never seen it like this. Even when he had gone to Margate it had been cloudy and dull and dark green. He had long since decided that the picture postcards were deliberately coloured up, that they were only a bit of pretend to send back to people at home.

Now the sky was lightening to blue – a paler, brighter blue than the sea, dotted with the occasional cottonwool cloud, white and fluffy.

In all their time in the boat this was the first morning that Jimmy had not woken to tossing waves, leaden skies and the bruising, buffeting of the boat.

The sun warmed the lumpy stuffing of his life jacket and, as he warmed, Jimmy's spirits rose.

"It's lovely, Sidney. Have a look."

Sidney slowly turned his head sideways. He didn't smile, but when he turned to look at Jimmy his eyes were brighter and had lost their dullness.

Keith was squinting into the sunlight and rubbing his eyes.

"Hot enough?" George said.

"I wish I had my glasses."

"Always gloomy, ain't you, Keith? Give it a break. At least you've got eyes, 'aven't you?"

Keith chuckled. It wasn't often that Keith laughed.

"George, Jimmy, let's get the awning down," said

Miss Cavendish. "We should get the benefit of this sun while we have it."

The awning folded and put away, they could sit straight at last and stretch their arms above their heads. Daniel, Jacob and Elizabeth were hauled out of the locker and sat in the sunlight.

"What are you up to, George?" shouted Jimmy.

George was edging himself up on the side of the boat, swinging his legs over.

"What are you doing?"

"Washing me feet. Giving my toes a swim . . ."

"Well, why not," said Miss Cavendish cheerfully. "You can all sit on the edge and dangle your feet, except Sidney of course."

It was wonderful to unfurl his cramped legs, stretch his confined feet and stretch his toes. Jimmy watched his toes wriggling in the water like little pink fish. He loved the trail of silvery ripples their movements made. But now the pink fish were abruptly attacked by bigger, bonier pink fish with sharp teeth.

"Get your feet off, George!" said Jimmy. "And it's about time you cut your toenails!"

"We'll all need a good scrub and brush up when we arrive," laughed Miss Cavendish.

When they arrived . . . But there was no wind filling the sails. They were hardly moving. Occasionally the sail flapped lazily, but it didn't billow with wind and bear them along in the brisk way it had the day before.

Jimmy stared at the sea. They weren't going to get

there very fast. He was too tired and lulled by the sun to work that one out now. He stared into the blue, cool water. He was so thirsty! The water was so welcoming, so inviting . . . He could slip down into it, allow its soft wetness to slake his parched body, sink down into endless water, down and down, never reaching the bottom . . .

No, he mustn't. He'd go mad if he did, if he drank that water. The chief steward had told them again and again to resist the temptation. Jimmy stared anxiously at Daniel and Jacob. He knew what they might be thinking too.

"We mustn't drink it," he said firmly. "It 'ud kill us."

Jimmy's harsh words jolted them out of their dreaming.

"Course I wasn't going to drink it, stupid," said George blinking hard.

Elizabeth had the shocked and trembling face of a cornered mouse, so Jimmy knew what had been in her mind too.

At midday the chief steward brought round tinned salmon on the usual hard, dry biscuit. None of the boys touched their biscuits.

"I'll keep it and have me water first," said Jimmy cheerfully.

"There's no water, son," said the chief steward quietly. "From now on we'll have water once – in the evening."

No water! Jimmy couldn't believe it. He felt he was dying of thirst, but he was never in such a bad way as Sidney. He stared at the chief steward in despair.

"Listen boys," the steward spoke carefully, as if each word was an effort to get out. "You've got pyjama buttons . . ." The boys leant forward, listening intently. "Suck your pyjama buttons – it'll help with the thirst."

When the steward had gone Jimmy crammed his biscuit into his pocket along with Sidney's. They might as well have tried to eat a stone as munch the dry biscuit in their swollen mouths. Slowly he tugged his pyjama collar above his life jacket and fumbled for the top button.

It tasted salty to begin with, but that soon went. At first it helped the thirst, but not for long. It was a trick, Jimmy could see that. The sucking kidded you at first, until your body worked out it was a sham.

"Jimmy . . ."

It was Sidney. He hadn't spoken since his torments of the previous night.

"It's all right, Sidney," said Jimmy quickly. He couldn't bear him to start up yelling and screaming again.

"Jim . . ."

"Now don't you worry. You just lie there and get a nice bit of this sun."

"Jim . . ."

"It'll warm you up in no time. Lie down, settle down – you're doing fine there."

Sidney lay out on his back on top of the locker, while the boys sat in front of him, dangling their legs in the sparkling sea and basking in the sunshine.

"Look . . ." Sidney was struggling to lift his weak arm.

"Now don't fuss yourself . . ." All the boys turned to watch Sidney. Miss Cavendish smiled anxiously from the other side of the locker.

A scraggy arm emerged from the rising pyjama sleeve. Jimmy tried to press it gently back.

"No," said George. "Leave 'im. 'E's up to somethin'."

George watched the arm as it rose shakily. His gaze continued up, beyond it to the sky. George stared and grabbed Jimmy's arm.

"What's 'e seen."

Jimmy looked up reluctantly. He didn't want to see any more of Sidney's visions – not after the prison bars of last night.

"Sidney!" George roared. "It's a plane, 'ent it?"

Jimmy stared and stared. He couldn't believe his eyes, but there were no clouds up there this time, nothing to trick the eye. A speck was growing in the sky, and in the still air Jimmy could just hear a faint drone.

"Airplane?"

"It's an airplane!"

The cry swept like wildfire from one end of the boat to another. Petty Officer Hamilton stumbled to the mast and ran the white petticoat up the masthead. Everyone was shouting and craning their necks skyward.

"I hope they see us," said Keith. "It's extremely difficult to spot a tiny boat in an enormous expanse of sea from way up there." He peered up and shaded his eyes.

"It's big . . . and it's got little windows along the side," shouted Jimmy.

"I expect it's a Sunderland – a flying-boat – that's what it will be," said Keith.

"A Sunderland is it? 'Spect yer goin' to tell us next it ain't possible to get a Sunderland out here in the middle of the Atlantic," said George sarcastically.

"Well, it is almost impossible. It must be a freak chance for a flying-boat on patrol in the Atlantic to be over this way, but I . . ."

The flying-boat had seen them. It dived straight at them and then swooped above them, flying in a low circle, like some cumbersome beetle. It was a huge, noisy plane, with a row of windows along each side. As it dipped past them, Jimmy saw the head of the pilot, encased in a leather flying helmet and goggles. The pilot wound down his window and waved.

Jimmy's arm weighed a ton, but he waved as he never had before.

"All right, Sidney? Now don't you try . . ."

The boys waved and shouted so much that their excitement made them forget their thirst and exhaustion. Round and round flew the plane. Then it was off, away over the sea, until it faded beyond the horizon.

They chattered with excitement, but it was nervous chatter, about everything and nothing.

The Sunderland had had no markings on it. What if it wasn't English? What if it was a German pilot in a captured British flying-boat? Could they have imagined it, an hallucination like the land on the horizon? The doubts raced into Jimmy's mind as fast as he tried to chase them away. He didn't voice them, but he guessed he wasn't alone in thinking them, so they chatted about being a pilot, what their boat looked like from up there, and whether the sun was hotter, higher up.

A cheer went up when the second Sunderland appeared. Jimmy didn't know how long it had been since the first, but it felt like hours. The plane circled twice, flying lower and lower. A door opened in its side and something was thrown out, landing in the sea with a great splash, and then the Sunderland roared its engines and climbed into the sky and disappeared.

"Point at the drop," shouted Lieutenant Ingram. "Keep all eyes skinned for the drop."

"Good thing there ain't no waves," said Jimmy gleefully to George.

He pointed at the bobbing parcel the size of a grocery box. In waves they'd been through over the past week, they would never have seen, let alone found, the drop.

The men at the tiller struggled to pull the boat round, until she gradually shifted her course. Other men, on the handles, yanked back and forwards, but they were weak and each pull was an enormous effort.

"Keep pointing," shouted Lieutenant Ingram.

The gunner and Petty Officer Hamilton climbed on to the back of the boat, tore off their life jackets and dived overboard. Jimmy, George and Keith stood at the gunwhale and pointed at the drop floating in and out of view, as the men swam away on the waves. The men glanced behind them from time to time to check their course against the pointing hands.

They swam slowly and laboriously to the bundle. Even the gunner was not the swimmer he once had been. Then they swam back, towing the box behind them, until, exhausted and dripping, they were hauled grinning over the stern of the boat.

It was agonising watching Lieutenant Ingram cut the rope that bound the Mae West jacket to the parcel. Then he had to cut off the parcel's oilskin coating.

"Blimey!" shouted George. "Look what 'e's got!"

Jimmy saw the lieutenant grin and raise up an armful of tins.

"It's food, Sidney. They've sent us some food!"

The tins were turned over to the chief steward.

Music, jolly mouth-organ music, drifted down the boat. The gunner's head jerked up and down as he blew into his tightly cupped hands.

"I never knew the gunner had a mouth organ,"

laughed Jimmy. "He's playin' one of Dad's old songs! 'Pack up your Troubles in your Old Kitbag'. That's a funny thing to bring alone when you're shipwrecked, a mouth organ. Eh, Sidney – you still got my lucky shrapnel?"

A look of panic flashed across Sidney's face and he struggled to raise his head.

"No, you lie back – I'll look."

George and Keith joined Jimmy and all three crouched over Sidney. Jimmy edged his hands under Sidney's life jacket and scrabbled up the material of his jacket. His fingers felt as if they were crawling up some sharp, pronged ladder. Each of Sidney's ribs stuck out painfully; there was nothing to him but skin and bone. But sharpest of all, digging uncomfortably between his ribs, was the nobbly, hard outline of cold metal.

"That must have hurt," said Jimmy as he pulled out the blackened metal. "You shouldn't have kept it so close."

"Lucky . . ." The faint word escaped Sidney's lips.

"That's right," said Jimmy triumphantly. "It is lucky – and we're goin' to be all right!"

CHAPTER THIRTEEN

Lieutenant Ingram held up his hand and gradually the singing died down along the boat.

"Thank you, ladies and gentlemen, boys and girls – a fine performance!"

A gale of laughter exploded in the boat. George drummed so fiercely with his fists on the locker top that Sidney jumped.

"Watch out, George," said Jimmy. "We can't have Sidney droppin' off into the sea!"

Keith blinked as he tried to make out what Lieutenant Ingram was up to.

"We have been spotted," continued the lieutenant, "and I feel I can at last say we are about to be rescued. I have a note here, in the drop, which says a destroyer is in the area. At present the destroyer is only forty miles away, waiting for a convoy returning from Canada . . ."

He wasn't able to finish, his words drowned by cheers.

". . . and now I will ask the steward to serve lunch."

There were tins of fruit, salmon, and beans in tomato sauce. They used their open hands as plates and bowls, licking every bit of peach or tomato sauce clean off their palms.

Jimmy couldn't persuade Sidney to eat, but the chief steward gave him a tin with peach juice in, and Jimmy poured it drop by drop into Sidney's mouth.

"What about the water then?" asked Jimmy as the steward came round yet again with freshly opened tins. "Sidney here has got to have some water. I might get 'im to have a bite then too."

"Sorry, son, you know the rule – water ration at night only."

"Come on," complained George. "The destroyer'll be here in a couple of hours, Lieutenant Ingram said so."

"We aren't rescued yet, son. It's my job to conserve the water. There'll be enough drink when we are picked up."

George groaned as the chief steward moved away.

"He's right," said Keith. "The destroyer could be attacked by a submarine before it reaches us. Survival rules must be followed until the point of rescue."

"Oh yeah," sneered George. "I suppose you've worked it out that we're on a submarine route."

"There aren't 'routes'. U-boats patrol at random until they lock on to a ship . . ."

"I'll lock on to you if you keep up this joyful news," snorted George. "These peaches are good, ain't they, Jimmy? I've never 'ad a white peach, I bet they're pricey. Fancy having a white peach, Keith?"

With Sidney cared for, Jimmy stared at his own hands. In one palm he cradled beans in tomato sauce, while in the other lay half a juicy, gleaming pear. It was a difficult decision, so he took little tentative licks at both.

It seemed an age of eating and chatting, with the sun arching across the sky, before the destroyer came in sight. Sleek and grey, she bristled like a hedgehog with guns and turrets. Black smoke steamed from her funnels as she raced towards them from the horizon with astonishing speed.

"I hope she's goin' to stop," said Jimmy anxiously.

He clutched Sidney as the big ship bore down on them. He was sure they were going to collide, but the destroyer came around, and hove to within a few yards of their lifeboat. It was a beautiful manoeuvre, like some grey top spinning and stopping to order in front of them.

Dark-uniformed sailors ran around on deck, responding to shouted orders. They threw down lines which the gunner and Petty Officer Hamilton caught and tied fast to the lifeboat.

The boys were struggling to stand.

"Wait!"

It was the voice of Miss Cavendish, a frightened, terrified voice.

"We're not rushing," said Jimmy indignantly.

"Father O'Brien – did you hear that?" whispered

Miss Cavendish frantically. "Did you hear it – 'herren'?"

"Oh dear, Miss Cavendish. Do you think . . . ?"

" 'Herr' means mister or man, does it not, Father O'Brien, so 'herren' means men?"

"I don't speak German, Miss Cavendish, but I believe you are right – 'herr' is like the French 'monsieur'."

Jimmy listened to the shouting. Miss Cavendish was right. He could hear 'herren' every now and again too. But he could hear English shouts too, or at least they sounded like an odd sort of English.

Jimmy turned to Keith, who was also listening intently, and saw a smile flicker slowly across his face.

"Come on, Keith. Is she right?"

Jimmy, George and Sidney waited anxiously for Keith to reply.

"I don't know German," Keith said, "but I think it's Scottish. It's a Scottish accent and they are referring to the stern."

George stood still and listened. Then he turned and thumped Keith on the back.

"That's the best thing you've said in days."

Above them, crowding over the deck rails, was a line of grinning faces. Jimmy smiled thankfully back.

"That's a wee lassie down there!" came a shout.

"There's kiddies in that boat!"

Two sailors came down rope ladders and made their way along the boat to the bows.

"Come along, lassie," said a big sailor with sandy hair. He lifted Elizabeth in his freckled arms as effortlessly as if she were a feather, "What's wrong wi' your arm then?"

Elizabeth was carried up the ladder and handed into the arms of the waiting sailors.

"The sick boy next," shouted the officer superintending from above.

"You'll have to carry Sidney," said Jimmy to a sunburnt sailor with huge, muscly arms. "His feet are somethin' terrible."

"I'll carry him gentle as a wean," smiled the sailor.

He scooped Sidney up in one careful movement and seemed astonished at how light he was, but it took two men to get Sidney up the ladder.

"Straight off to sick bay," ordered the officer as Sidney was helped over the rails. "Now the other boys!"

There was a little more space in the boat now Elizabeth and Sidney were gone, and even more after Jacob and Daniel had been carried up. Jimmy could scarcely believe it when it was his turn to go.

He struggled to his feet, but he couldn't stand. George was flailing around wildly too, holding on to the side of the boat. Keith got up and slowly slumped back into his seat.

Jimmy tried again. He had to get off! He couldn't be

left behind. He struggled up only to collapse again. He must make an effort. He couldn't be left . . .

Strong arms grabbed him under his armpits and he felt himself being lifted into the air. He was travelling down the boat. He weighed a ton usually, but he was being carried as if he weighed no more than a little kid. Up he swung, passed from hand to hand up the ladder. All around him were grinning faces, white teeth, one with a gold cap.

"You's OK now, laddie."

"Holiday's over, son."

"You's in the navy now."

"Take the boy down to sick bay," came an authoritative voice.

Someone handed Jimmy a tin mug. He grabbed it and rushed the water to his mouth, spilling half down his life jacket on the way. In gulp after gulp he drained it down. He wanted more, and more . . .

"No more, son – not till the doctor sees you."

The doctor's forehead was furrowed with anxious lines, while his hands fingered the stethoscope at the neck of the white coat over his naval officer's uniform.

"Mm . . . water, little and often, as much as he needs. But food – we need to be careful. His digestive system will be in a bad way from dehydration. Perhaps start with a few spoonfuls of porridge and we'll see how it goes from there."

171

The nursing orderly standing beside the doctor nodded and wrote notes on a pad.

"Their feet have experienced a degree of frostbite – "

"My feet are fine, mister," interrupted Jimmy. "It was just getting off that boat. I've stood up now."

"Yes . . ." said the doctor thoughtfully.

He took off the stethoscope, folded it neatly and slipped it back into the wide pocket of his coat.

"Are my instructions understood, Corporal Campbell?"

The orderly stood up straight and brought his heels together.

"Yessir."

Jimmy lay back on his bunk. Sheets! He lay on clean, white sheets, and he could stretch out every limb. He turned over and stared into George's dark eyes.

"It's all right!"

"It is," agreed George, and they both grinned.

"You all right over there, Keith?" Jimmy yelled to the bed beside the door.

Keith picked up a pair of glasses that lay on his pillow. They were too large to sit on his nose but he held them up to his eyes. "I can see you from here, Jimmy," he said with delight.

The three boys lay flat on their backs, exhausted.

As soon as they had got to the sick bay, the medical orderly had told them to undress. It had taken Jimmy an age just to untie the ribbons of his life jacket. His fingers wouldn't do what he wanted them to do and he couldn't remember how you untied a knot. Life jacket off, the buttons of his pyjamas were too fiddly. How did you get a button through that slit, and which arm came first out of the jacket sleeve, and how did you bend the arm to slip the jacket off? Nothing seemed simple any longer. It was like working out some complicated mechanical operation without instructions.

Now they were in new men's pyjamas. Jimmy hadn't a clue what to do about the flapping legs and arms, until the orderly went round them all in turn and rolled the ends up at wrists and ankles.

"Where's Sidney?"

"I dunno, Jimmy," said George.

Without Sidney to look after, Jimmy felt as if he had one limb missing.

"They took Father O'Brien and one of the Lascars off too. They're all of them poorly," added Keith.

"We'll find him tomorrow then."

"We will."

They drifted into a deep dreamless sleep. Jimmy had never in his life felt so tired. He woke up from time to time to grab another glass of water from the carafe beside him. One time the carafe was empty, and he got up in a panic and stumbled to the door of the cabin. He was so thirsty – they were rationing the water!

"I've gotta have some. I can't wait to evenin'."

The surprised orderly led him back to his bunk.

"Of course you can have some, son." Jimmy heard

the soothing gurgle of the carafe filling up. "You can have all you like."

Jimmy drained the glass and slept.

Jimmy wasn't sure where he was when he woke. He was lost in space — no poking limbs and bodies pressed bonily close together.

He sat up. In the bed beside him a tuft of dark hair, washed and silky, sprouted from a sheet.

"George — you awake?"

They woke Keith. By each bed lay a pile of folded clothes. They pulled on the men's vests and over the top drew on thick seamen's sweaters.

"Look at me legs!" exclaimed Jimmy.

He looked down at the bruised, bony legs poking out from under the sweater that almost reached to his knees.

"Where've they gone?" said Jimmy in wonder. "They've shrunk."

"Not as thin as Sidney's, I'll bet," said George.

"Sidney! Let's go and look for 'im," said Jimmy. "He'll want a bit of company."

All three slipped out of their cabin. The first door in the passage opened easily. There were two beds and each one had an occupant, a long occupant. A brown hand lay motionless on the white sheet of one of the beds, while on the sheet of the opposite bed lay a pale hand with some beads entwined in the fingers.

"It's a rosary for praying," Keith whispered. "It must be Father O'Brien."

"Is that you, Keith," a tired voice came from the pillow.

"Yes, Father."

"Remember to thank the Lord, and tell all the boys to pray . . ."

"Yes, Father."

They closed the door quietly.

The next door they opened had only one bed in it with a sort of tent apparatus at its foot. They were about to close the door when there was a movement from the bedsprings.

"Jimmy – is that you?"

The three boys burst into the room. Sidney was protruding from the far end of the tent, propped up on the pillows. He looked very pale and thin, but he smiled.

"What's all this about then?" grinned Jimmy. He was delighted to see Sidney again, especially a Sidney who smiled and talked. "How d'ya manage a first-class cabin on yer own? They put us back in cabin class!"

"They've taken off two of me toes," said Sidney, pointing to the tent contraption over his feet.

"Get 'em back then!" growled George. "They can't just take bits off you without askin'!"

"They was bad – frostbite. They 'ad to take 'em off or the others would've gone bad too. I'll be able to run again, the doctor's promised, when they're better."

"That's right," said Jimmy. "You'll be as good as new. I'll race you. I'm that skinny now, Sidney, I might even be able to keep up with you."

"There are very good artificial limbs designed these days," said Keith holding up his giant glasses, "but I haven't heard of artificial toes. That would be an interesting problem . . ."

"Don't you worry, Sidney," said George, "with old clever clogs 'ere. Keith'll fix you up with some, won't you, Keith?"

"Well, I'm not sure . . ."

"Out, boys!" The orderly stood in the doorway, frowning. "Sidney is recovering from his anaesthetic and needs peace and quiet!"

They raced off round the ship. No one stopped them. They even went down to the kitchens where the cook filled up a big steel cooking bowl with tinned fruit. The boys watched as tin after tin was opened. On top he poured a giant tin of condensed milk.

"Who's that for?" George asked.

The cook didn't answer but fetched three spoons from a drawer.

"OK, lads, tuck in."

"But the doctor said —" began Keith.

"A bit of honest food never hurt anyone," said the cook.

Jimmy wasn't inclined to argue. They seized the spoons and shovelled the fruit down. It was delicious!

Then they took it in turns to pick up the bowl and sip the remaining juice.

Later the captain allowed them to visit the bridge and they were shown, on the navigation charts, where they had been picked up, five hundred miles out into the Atlantic. As the day wore on and they steamed at speed further east, they sighted other vessels.

It was the trees that finally convinced Jimmy. Land came into view and he could distinctly make out their shapes. And as the destroyer slowly drew nearer the trees became greener and their trunks browner. It was the first solid bit of land, and the trees looked like something rooted and firm, something that didn't toss and roll.

"Seen the trees, George?" said Jimmy pointing.

"Yeah."

Keith clutched his glasses to his eyes.

"This isn't the Mersey estuary," he said. "There are islands and hills here."

"You're right, lad," said the voice of the sailor behind him. "We're coming up the Clyde."

"Where we goin'?" said Jimmy.

"Gourock. We're in Scotland."

Jimmy and George stared at Keith. Scotland – Keith had been right all along!

Keith shuffled under their gaze, rubbed his glasses on the sleeve of his sweater and gazed out at the islands.

George gave Keith a shove.

"No need to show off," he said.

"He's not said a word," said Jimmy indignantly.

Keith grinned happily.

The destroyer followed the pilot ship up the wide river until she was edged into berth.

"Look at that crowd down there," said Jimmy, peering over the railings. "There's photographers down there. Look at that bloke with all those cameras."

"We must have someone important on board," said Keith. "They look like press photographers."

They peered round to look, but there was no one behind them. Someone below had seen them and was shouting up at them.

"Boys! This way – wave! That's right! And again!"

Jimmy stared in amazement, his eyes scanning the grinning, waving crowd and the flashing light bulbs. Were they really being photographed? He searched the faces below. At the back . . . Yes, there at the back. Someone who stood still, watching not waving, someone with a smudged face and coal-grimed overalls, someone who stood apart from the long beige mackintoshes of the pressmen and the dark uniforms of the sailors.

"Dad!" he shouted. "It's me – Jimmy!"

His father stared as if he had seen a ghost, and then he turned away.

"As soon as I heard, Jimmy, I came. I was in Glasgow with a trainload of troops, and the station master told me he'd heard on the radio a boat from the *Karachi* 'ad been found, and they thought yer name was on the list."

"What did Mum say?"

"I don't know. I sent a message to the shop – they've got a telephone – and I asked Mrs Edwards to take a message round to your mum."

Jimmy was sitting in the lounge of the hotel at Gourock to which they had been taken. His father sat opposite him. From time to time his father put out a hand and patted Jimmy on the knee or his shoulder as if to reassure himself that Jimmy was really there.

"Dad – I've got this friend Sidney. He's in a bad way, they've taken off two of his toes, but he's really worried about seein' his mum again."

"Why's that, Jimmy?"

"He promised he'd look after his little sister. He couldn't have – there wasn't time, Dad."

"Of course there wasn't . . ."

"Where did the other kids get to? Then I can tell Sidney."

"There weren't many other kids, Jimmy. They got a destroyer out as quick as they could but that took a day or so. They'd mostly all gone by then, apart from a handful of grown-ups, and a few older kids who were strong enough to put up with the cold."

"Died?"

"Some didn't make the boats. With the ones that did, it was the waves, swamped the boats they did. They was full of water, cold water up to their waists.

They got too cold. You were lucky, Jimmy, very lucky."

They had to stay one more night in the hotel before they were allowed to travel.

"It weren't just luck," said Jimmy to Keith and George as they lay in bed. "They were good sailors – Lieutenant Ingram, Petty Officer Hamilton, Gunner Mackenzie, the Lascars and the chief steward. We had more than a bit of luck on our boat."

They were silent for a moment. Jimmy thought of Mr Barry and his racing car, and of Babs proudly showing him her purse, and kindly Pat and little Jean with her new china doll. It wasn't fair.

"I'm goin' back with me dad tomorrow. What's happening to you, Keith?"

"I'm going to stay with this cousin of my father's. I've never met him, but he got in touch with the welfare people after I had left. He'd only just heard about the bombing, but he was too late."

"You look pleased enough. Is 'e all right then?"

"He's a bit old, but he and his wife have no children so they've got room for me."

Jimmy felt sorry for Keith going to an elderly couple with no children.

"He's a professor, though," explained Keith cheerfully.

"A professor?" said George.

"Someone who teaches in a university. He teaches engineering."

"You'll be all right then," said Jimmy. "You'd better get 'im to help with those toes for Sidney."

"I'm not sure . . ."

"How about you, George?" said Jimmy. "Are you goin' to try Canada again."

"Don't mind," muttered George.

"Where you goin' then?"

"They 'aven't decided."

'*They*' decided.

"George has been found a place in an orphanage for boys in Glasgow, Dad. They say it's for the time bein', but he'll probably be movin' later."

"Will he, Jimmy?"

"An' we've got a spare bed at home."

"We have, Jimmy. This George – he a mate of yours, is he then?"

"Yes – he is."

"You'd better bring 'im along, then."

That morning their pictures were in all the papers.

BOYS BROUGHT BACK FROM THE DEAD
AMAZING SURVIVAL AT SEA
TORPEDOED CHILDREN SAVED

The boys sat on Sidney's bed and read them.

"We're famous!" said Jimmy.

"Course we are!" said Sidney.

Sidney smiled and laughed. He'd spoken to his mum on the telephone and she was coming, with four of his brothers and sisters, to fetch him. Keith had glanced at the papers but had put them aside in favour of a book called *Nine Engineering Wonders of the World, Explained with Full Illustrations*.

Only George sat silent and uneasy.

"How will yer mum know I'm comin'?" he said suddenly. "Mebbe she won't want me."

"Dad will get the message to her," said Jimmy cheerfully. "Look at this, George – you're grinnin' like a cat in this one."

Jacob and Daniel were collected by a man with a beard in a long black coat and wide black hat, who hugged and kissed them when they flew into his arms.

Elizabeth's grandmother arrived in a very large black car driven by a very old chauffeur.

"Rolls Royce," said Keith. "They must have used up all their petrol ration for weeks!"

"I'll send you a postcard from Gloucestershire," Elizabeth said to Jimmy. "I'm going to stay with my grandparents."

"Tell your grandad, if he needs a spot of help on his yacht, I've got experience, I have."

"Oh – I will, Jimmy."

Jimmy smiled. Elizabeth's face was white and tear-stained and she was dressed all in black, with black shiny shoes. Her mother had not been found.

Jimmy, George and his father travelled third class on the train to Glasgow, changed for a train to Liverpool and then changed at Liverpool on to a London train. Jimmy was tired. The excitement had masked his exhaustion, but now every part of him ached and hurt. George sat tense and quiet and never said a word, so Jimmy supposed he was tired too.

Dad didn't bother them with questions, but kept looking at Jimmy as if to reassure himself that his son existed.

When they got to London's King's Cross Station, they transferred to the underground. Jimmy's feet hurt so much that he hobbled along, clutching George's and his father's arms.

They got out at Riverside Station and Jimmy could hardly bear to put his feet down on the platform.

"I don't think I'm goin' to make it, Dad."

"Course you will, son." said Dad.

"Mr Smith," said George, "you take the bags and I'll 'elp Jimmy."

"Are you sure?"

"Yeah – I can manage."

Jimmy's father picked up the bulging bags full of presents and clothes that the boys had been given, and the triple pocket money Baron Wolcinski had handed out before he left. He was laden from head to foot. George backed up to Jimmy, grabbed him and swung

Jimmy across his back. So that was how he had carried Keith!

They edged their way slowly out of the station.

"Eh! Mr Smith! Is that your kid off the *Karachi*?"

It was Mr Edwards in his apron, standing outside his greengrocer's shop.

" 'Old on. You can't carry 'im 'ome like that – not after what 'e's been through."

Mr Edwards slipped back into the shop.

"Mavis! Mavis! Close up for me, luv. I'm takin' Mr Smith's lad off the *Karachi* 'ome in the van."

A little crowd of curious people had gathered outside.

"It's Jimmy Smith," someone whispered.

"Oh no!" said another voice in a shocked tone.

The van smelt of cabbage and onions and potatoes. They drove down Middle Lane, past craters in the road, and the charred remains of bombed-out houses, side by side with untouched houses with lacy curtains behind taped-up windows, and flowers still in pots on windowsills.

The van turned up Union Street and stopped at number 35. George helped Jimmy out, and between George and Dad they got him up the front steps. The door was open into the kitchen, and the table laid for tea. Jimmy had never seen such a spread – potted meat, cold boiled potatoes, lettuce, scones and cakes.

"Where'd Mum get this lot, Dad?" he said in

184

amazement. No one could get that much with wartime rationing.

His father hesitated and then laughed.

"It's left over from yer funeral tea!"

"My funeral!"

"We had it two days ago, a sort of memorial funeral. Yer Mum insisted we held out a bit, even though they told us you was drowned for sure. But we couldn't avoid it in the end. The neighbours all chipped in, see."

Jimmy surveyed the table.

"It must have bin a feast," he said at last. "You could've waited for me!"

His father had turned away to the shelf above the range. He pulled down a white card, edged with a black border.

"There you are Jimmy!" he said with a chuckle that came close to a sob.

Jimmy examined the smart, printed card.

JAMES SMITH.

Born April 25, 1929

Lost at sea, September 13, 1940.

Beloved only child of Reginald and Ethel Smith

"O hear us when we cry to Thee,
For those in peril on the sea."

"Yer mum insisted on it," said Jimmy's father, wiping at his eyes with the back of his hand. "She wanted it all done proper."

Astonished, Jimmy examined the card. "Take a look at this, George!"

But George was staring at the table, his eyes moving round the plates neatly set out on the oilcloth. Someone had laid the table and there were four places.

"See, George," said Jimmy. "She's expectin' you."

George's face softened and for the first time that day he grinned at Jimmy. Then he stared over Jimmy's head at something in the doorway.

Jimmy turned and Mum was standing there.

He didn't need to smile at Mum. She knew. Then she was beside him, running her fingers through his tufty hair, and he didn't mind.

"Well, Jimmy," she said at last. "Time we had our tea." She lifted the kettle from the range and poured boiling water into the teapot. "So we ain't done so bad now – sent one away and got two back."

Based on a True Story

Sea of Peril is a novel, but it is based on true events surrounding the sinking of the ship *Benares* in 1940. Ninety children were on board, en route for Canada as government sponsored evacuees. Of this number, only thirteen were saved, including six boys who survived eight days in a lifeboat in the Atlantic.

The children in *Sea of Peril*, who are the main characters of the story – Jimmy, Sidney, Keith, George, Elizabeth, Jacob and Daniel – are entirely fictional characters and bear no resemblance to actual people.

While the original lifeboat from the *Benares* had six boys on board, there was in addition a considerable contingent of Lascars, a gunner, a Roman Catholic priest, a lady children's escort, a Polish shipping-line director, a young cadet, a steward, and the fourth officer of the *Benares*. These characters have been recreated in fictional form, and play minor roles.

The author wishes to acknowledge two books, both out of print, used as reference: *Atlantic Ordeal: the story of Mary Cornish* by Elspeth Huxley (Chatto and Windus, 1941), and *Children of the* Benares by Ralph Barker (Methuen, 1987).

The author would like to thank Mike Donnelly of the Liverpool Maritime Museum for his help with research.

An especial thanks is owed to Derek Capel, Paul Shearing and Freddie Steels, who were among the original six boys in the *Benares* lifeboat, and who generously gave the author their time to recall memories of their ordeal.